The River's Edge

BY J. G. JAKES

xulon
PRESS

The River's Edge

by J.G. Jakes

Printed in the United States of America

Edited by Xulon Press

ISBN 9781498410090

www.xulonpress.com

TABLE OF CONTENTS

Chapter 1

CREEL BURR

$\mathcal{T}$he flames from the hobos' fire danced in the still of the night. The burning embers in the hot coals crackled and popped. Huddled close to the warmth of the fire was an old hobo, about fifty in age. He and his comrades, wrapped in dingy gray wool blankets pulled tightly around their necks, made their nightly abode in the low-lying gully beneath the train trusses. They would sleep there until the next train passed, usually after midnight on the first and third Monday of the month. This was the third Monday, and it was almost midnight.

Suddenly, the vagabond with a red bandana sat upright. On this cool, crisp night, perspiration beaded his dirty, unkempt face. He yanked his bandana from around his neck, feverishly wiping the sweat from his brow. His tense, rigid body shivered. Dark, mysterious eyes darted from one sleeping companion to the next. Had they heard his groaning caused by a terrifying nightmare? No. Everyone was sleeping peacefully. He was the only soul wakened by the agonizing sounds and thrashing about caused by a tormented sleeper. Thankfully, the old drifter's secret wailings of fragmented memories that had plagued him since he was a young child remained unnoticed.

The horrifying nightmares were always the same. A small, frail boy, about five years in age, trapped in a small, cluttered storage room, and frightened of the big man—a loathsome, burly figure with bushy eyebrows and a nauseating stench. The disgusting man reached for the terrified and powerless young boy, who had nowhere to run, nowhere to hide. The child fiercely fought to free himself, but to no avail. A wicked smile etched its way across the face of the man with the demonic character. The child continued to struggle, knowing, as usual, he was doomed. The hefty man pushed the terrified, small child onto a croaker sack filled with some sort of beans as he pulled ragged, gray pants down to the trapped child's knees. Trembling, tiny fingers dug deep into the coarse, thick fiber of the brown bean sack. Holding on tightly and clenching his teeth, the entrapped boy prepared for his inevitable fate, a fate that found its crooked path to his defenseless, ill-treated body as it had so many times before.

Diminutive and powerless, the young boy felt worthless. After all, who was he? Only a poor, forsaken child orphaned at birth, left on the doorstep at a quaint Jacksonville orphanage. No one valued him. No one wanted him, and no one loved him. His only use in this world was to be the prey for the sexually per-verted appetite of the director of the orphanage, the brawny man whom he despised, with the stench he found repulsive.

Hatred filled this tiny, vulnerable heart. Tears of sorrow welled in the child's eyes and rolled down his cheeks, leaving wet trails of abomination and shame. This nobody's child had a name. His name was Creel...Creel Burr.

Suddenly, a log on the hobos' fire crumbled and fell into the center of the burning coals. Sparks danced, flickering upwards into the darkness. Startled, Creel snapped back from dark, deep thoughts to present reality. The remembered dream would soon fade into the obscurity of the night and slink back into the depths of his soul. For sure, another night, another campfire, it would return. With it, the bitterness and abhorrence would revisit the heart of this rogue of a hobo. A terrible angst was beginning to boil from the pit of his being, a crippling tide of panic and dread. Feelings of self-hatred, shame, and guilt held him bound in a petrified stage of hopelessness, the hopelessness of indifference.

The hobo's dark childhood had changed him into the mon-ster he was, a monster with dark desires. This young orphan boy was transformed into a hideous man, a man who became a pro-lific serial killer as he rode from rail to rail, victim to victim. A predictable yet disturbing routine had emerged—ride the rails by night, search for prey by day.

Creel reached into a knapsack that he carried with him as he rode the rails from town to town. Prowling like the animal he was, he fed his need for violence. From inside, he pulled out a cloth bag sewn from a flour sack and pulled tightly together by a drawstring.

"Huh," he mumbled. Urges began to arise along with the hatred festering in his heart, sexual urges—perverted, in fact! His dark personality, a result of his shady past, spurred the manifestation of wickedness. Unrelenting rage grew, as did his secret desire to sexually dominate his victims. The psychological thrill he received resulted in his continued killing spree, and more and more, it fulfilled his need to act out his violence.

Hoak Mann, arousing from his sleep, rubbed his crusty eyes and yawned. "What ya doing awake, Creel?"

Motionless, Creel stared into the fire. The fire's reflection glittered and danced in the dark of his eyes.

Hoak glanced at the other two hobos. Still undisturbed, both were resting quite comfortably. It appeared that no one was interested in catching the rails tonight. Hoak looked at Creel and then down at the flour-sack bag Creel clenched tightly in his hands.

"Ya got that look in your eye again, Creel." Hoak motioned towards the bag. "You get that look every time you pull that ol' ragged sack out. You hold it like it's got gold or something in it."

Hoak stood, brushing the dirt from his clothes. He walked away from the fire only a couple of steps, stopping momentarily to untie his pants. Relieving himself, he moaned a muffled, "Ah."

Creel's distorted face suddenly showed signs of apathy that would inevitably seethe into wrath as he viewed Hoak Mann with revulsion. He spat upon the ground and then wiped the dribbling saliva with the sleeve of his tattered and soiled shirt.

Hoak, not seeing the look of repugnance on Creel's face, continued with his badgering. "What is it that you always carry in that ol' sack, Creel?"

Grumbling, Creel stood. Hands still clenched by his side, his eyes narrowed and blazed with disgust. Slowly, he began to gather his meager belongings, wrapping them carefully inside his knapsack. Then he tied the brown croaker bag securely with a rope.

"Aw, come on now, Creel," began Hoak. A frown contorted his weathered and wrinkled face. "Every time I try to talk about anything, you get all bent out of shape, pout like a goat eatin' briars, and take off down the rails again."

In the distance was the rumbling of a railroad train chugging towards the trestle. Creel slung his sack over his shoulder. Never looking back, he scampered to the top of the small gully to the flat, smooth ground near the edge of the tracks. The big engine neared. The clanking of the steel wheels became louder and louder. In a brief moment, the engine passed. One boxcar, then another rolled by. Creel began to run. With one hand, he reached for the handle on the side of the boxcar. He pulled himself up and for a moment hung from the door's handle as his feet dangled. With a mighty heave, he dragged himself into the covered railway car. The powerful locomotive towing several boxcars clanged and clattered down the tracks.

Hoak Mann stared into the darkness until he could neither see nor hear the large mass of rumbling steel. It had disappeared into the gloomy, lonely night. So had Creel Burr!

The train rumbled down the track for what seemed like hours. As the dawn crested upon the horizon, Creel noticed he was not alone in the boxcar. In this year, 1933, the United States was at the onset of the Great Depression. During these poverty-stricken times, devastated families who could not afford train fare rode the rails in boxcars. Unemployed and evicted from their homes, thousands of homeless people across America were forced to look for jobs elsewhere or join family members in other towns. Huddled together in a corner of the car was such a family. Bleak and distraught faces showed their plight. Creel showed no empathy.

The rolling steam engine began to slow, an indication that a crossing was near. Creel quickly gathered his belongings. No smiles were exchanged between occupants, only fear from the weary family and antipathy from Creel Burr.

Creel lunged through the door and hit the ground rolling, finally tumbling to a stop. He stood momentarily, brushed himself off, and stared down the track until the train was only a blur. Through the woods he trudged. Later, he sat down to rest against a fallen log. Suddenly, his brow furrowed and head cocked to one side.

In the nearby woods, the sound of laughter echoed through the magnificent hardwood and long-leaf yellow pines of Southwest Georgia—the laughter of children. Creel smiled—a wicked, eerie smile! Creel Burr had found his bliss. However, an unfortunate child would soon find her nightmare.

Slowly, he edged his way closer and closer. Excitement grew as he discreetly lay hidden in the underbrush. There he watched and listened. Patiently, he waited. A foretaste of sorrow loomed.

Chapter 2

IMPRINTS

The splashing water on a warm spring day ushered in a time of bliss for friends who knew no heartache, only toil and sweat of the brow. The friends from McAllister's Lane, felt the comforting warmth under the glow of a golden sun. Filtering their way through where the treetops crossed, the balmy rays melted the goose bumps caused by the spring waters that had not yet warmed from the winter season.

Kathryn McAllister, more often called Katie, and her neighbor friend, Rosie O'Hara, pulled off their shoes and raced through the chilly, shallow waters at the river's edge, a river that meandered unimpeded next to the land called the McAllister farm.

Another friend, a young Negro boy named Benjamin Roosevelt Washington King, but called Son, knelt beside limestone rock catching caddisflies, an excellent bait sheltering among the rocks in the shallow water.

Rosie, the youngest of the three friends, called out, "Come, on, Son! You can catch bait later. For now, let's have some fun."

Nonchalantly, Son ignored Rosie's lighthearted attempts to distract his dutiful undertaking. Having fun was something he would enjoy. However, more important was the need to supply his family with an ample amount of fish for their evening meal. As soon as he caught enough bait, he began preparing fishing poles to set in the pliable ground around the sloughs. There, he thrust the poles in malleable mud and waited patiently for big fish to casually swim by and take a bite of the wriggling bait.

Son sat down on the deeply incised sand bank and dug his feet into the cool, damp soil. After patting the sand snugly over his bare feet, he gently pulled them out, leaving foot imprints, which youngsters referred to as frog houses.

Son, proud of the perfectly shaped trajectory of the foot holes left in the wet sand, called out to his female friends, "Come look, Katie! Come look, Rosie! You ain't never seen no frog houses this fine!"

Giggling, Rosie raced to Son. Not Katie. Often she became weary of Rosie's and Son's frivolousness. As with any seventeen year old girl on the brink of becoming a young woman, she found herself tiring easily of silly, almost childess games. Standing aloof, she watched as Rosie stood over Son, admiring his crude construction of mud frog houses.

"That's pretty good," laughed Rosie. "But you know what they say about mud houses, don't you, Son?"

"Naw. What do they say?" As he looked up into Rosie's face, young and without blemish, he noticed her reddish-blonde hair, loosely tied with a blue ribbon, had fallen across her blue eyes and glistened in the sun. His bright eyes beamed. Quickly, he diverted his attention elsewhere.

"You better stop lookin' at me that way, boy! Negro boys ain't suppose to look at white girls that way."

Quickly, Son diverted his attention elsewhere.

"That's better and this is what happens to mud houses," giggled Rosie. The soaked hem of her calico dress was drenched with water. She raised it.

Nearby, the impertinent marauder Creel Burr lurked. The contemptible man's excitement grew.

Holding the hem of her dress, Rosie squeezed the water onto Son's perfectly constructed frog houses. The destructive water flowed profusely onto his creation erected from the supple earth of the water's edge.

"Mud houses don't last," sneered Rosie. "They always fall down just like stick ones, Son—just like the house you live in."

"You ain't got no room to fun at me, Rosie!" bellowed Son. "You're just as poor as me!"

"You'd better wash your mouth out. I'll tell my pa that you were"—she giggled—"taking a shine to me. And he'll beat the living tar out of ya."A lusty laugh erupted. Rosie gathered up her dress and danced back into the cool water, which was almost as cool as her attitude.

The cruel, vile remarks cut deep into Son's sensitive heart. For a moment, he sat quietly gazing, forlorn, at the devastation at his feet.

From nearby, Katie observed the hurt on her friend's face. Quietly, she eased over and sat by his side. "Aw, come on now, Son. You are not going to let that scrawny little heifer's remark get you down. "

Rosie O'Hara, overhearing Katie's comment, jeered as she pouted and kicked up water. "I am no little heifer, Katie McAllister, and I don't think that I am better than nobody else!" She turned towards Katie and staunchly put her hands on her hips. "Answer me this. If we were not living in these godforsaken backwoods miles away from other people, would Son and you still be huntin' and fishin' buddies? Huh? Would you?"

Katie did not attempt to thwart Rosie O'Hara's efforts to belittle her devotion to Son and his family. She knew her commitment and dedication to the Kings was rested on a well-grounded understanding of the Bible that the ground was level at the foot of the cross. Afterall, the color of a man's skin didn't make him better or worse than anyone else. It was what's inside their hearts that made them worthwhile.

Son scoffed, "She makes me so mad, Katie. She always acts like she's better than me. "

Katie chuckled. "Well, she always acts like she's better than anyone in this neck of the woods. But we know better, don't we?"

She winked at Son, causing a smile to radiate from his smooth, brown face.

Son tried to communicate his feelings of admiration to the wistful Katie, whose friendship he esteemed so much. He asked, "How come you don't act like that, Katie? How come you're the only white person in these parts who makes this poor li'l ol' black boy feel like he is just as good as anybody else?"

"First of all, you are not some li'l ol' black boy. You are only a year younger than I am and you probably weigh at least fifty more pounds than I do!"

"But I ain't fat am I, Katie?"

Laughing, Katie pinched the skin around his slender waist. "No, just muscle."

"Stop joshin' and tell me why you're good to me and I'm just a nobody?"

Katie's compassionate words gave Son the assurance he needed. "Kindness is a simple, blessed thing, Son. It is the Lord's great plan that we all be friends and appreciate one another for each other's own greatest worth. And you, my dear friend, are as good as anyone else on this earth. And don't you ever forget it. Hear me?"

" How come you talk so ed...ed....uc..?"

"Educated?"

"Yeah! That's the word."

"After I finished school, my teacher wanted me to continue learning. She bring me books to read. She said that I am smart and inquistive, and maybe, if I kept reading, I would be smart enough to be a teacher like her."

"What's yur favorite kind of book to read?" asked Son.

Katie smiled as she replied, "You know, I think I love poetry the best."

"How come, Katie?"

"I don't know. I guess when you speak the words, they kinda roll right out of your mouth. Leaves a sweet taste. Almost like the taste of honey suckles."

"Would you teach me to read them books some time, Katie. Please?"

Katie realized that poverty and illiteracy had marked Son deeply since blacks were unschooled in their part of the world. Still, she prayed that one day Son would eventually escape the backward farm life and the cruel mockers who always put others down so they could stand taller than anyone else.

"Of course, I will. You are going to go far in this life, and one day you are going to make something of yourself!" Katie assured Son.

The two friends from different races lay down on the sandbar near the river's edge. Lazily, they watched Son's set poles for any tug on the line indicating a fish had been caught. In the quietness, the willows bent their long, green skirts into the water. The tops of the giant cypress swayed gracefully in the cool breeze.

Son tilted his head up towards the sky. "You know, Katie, dying and going to Heaven ain't gonna be that bad. You can drink from a fountain that never goes dry and live in a mansion high in the sky."

Katie burst into a jovial laugh. "See? I told you that you're going to make something of yourself. You're already a poet and didn't know it!"

"That's right. But you know what's gonna make Heaven really special?"

"I do, but let me hear your answer, Mr. Robert Frost."

"Who?"

"Never mind. What is going to make Heaven so special to you?"

"No more people picking on you 'cause they don't think that you're as good as they are. Yep, going to Heaven ain't gonna be that bad 'cause then I don't have to live in some ol' stick house!"

Katie stared intently at her dearest friend. She teased, "Gotta be a good boy to get that mansion!"

"How do I be good when sometimes I do things that make me bad?"

"Always take the right road."

"Right road? What do you mean?"

"Well, take McAllister's Lane for instance. Life is sorta like that ol' road. When you get to the end of the lane, there's a cross-road. One way goes to the left, one to the right. Just make sure that you always go *right*."

"Oh, I see. That sounds easy enough. Is that what you do, Katie? I mean, always walk the right road?"

"I do my best. I'd like to go to Heaven, too." Her voice softened, almost to a whisper. "I'd like to see my mother one day."

"That's right. You ain't ever seen your ma, have you, Kat? I mean 'cause she died when you were a baby."

"Yeah," Katie sighed. Although reconciled to the fact, being motherless still saddened the young, vulnerable girl from McAllister's Lane. She diverted to the ongoing conversation. "But anyway, to make my point, Heaven is the extent of the blessings God has planned for us. And we need to have the strength of character to take the right paths so we can have the blessings that we have been promised."

"You are so smart, Kat. Who taught you all this stuff? I mean about Heaven and all?"

"Your mother taught me! And she tried to teach you, but you were always too busy playing around to listen!"

Son chuckled. "Aw, you know how us boys are."

For a while, Son contemplated the things of Heaven and above. He asked, "When I do something bad, will you walk the road with me and get me straight? I don't like walking alone."

An endless promise was made, and a friendship was tightly bound. "You'll never walk the road alone," Katie said. "We'll always walk it together. That's what friends do."

Son smiled. Content in a bonded relationship with Katie, he knew she would never forsake him in times of trouble.

In the distance, a masked little bandit, a raccoon, was trying to torment an unconcerned frog. Katie giggled as she pointed to the raccoon. "I don't know about that fellow, but I'm getting mighty tired of eating frog legs and catfish stew. How about let's go hunting, Son, and leave that silly girl Rosie to herself? I'd rather have fried squirrel than fish on my supper plate tonight."

Son's elated face beamed. If there was anything that he enjoyed more than fishing with Katie, it was hunting. "You bet!" he exclaimed. "I'm getting tired of eating fish, too."

Suddenly, Son shrugged modestly. His dark brown eyes sparkled. "Katie, do you really think I'm going to be good enough to go to Heaven one day? Even if I'm a colored boy?" His eyes eagerly searched hers, looking for reassurance and hope.

"Of course! God doesn't look at our skin. And you're going to have a big, fine mansion to live in and not an ol' stick house that dissolves away like those silly old frog houses." Katie continued to encourage him. "Yes sir. And one day, Rosie O'Hara will eat her words. Have trust that everything will be made right. I don't understand why colored people are looked down upon, and it is sad that our world is like this. But I promise you, Son; if you put your trust in the good Master, He will set things right. You know, He has His hand in everything, and His promises are always true."

Son scuffed his feet and mumbled, "Think so, Katie?"

"Sure do! God cares. He really does. And He knows that there is a lot of suffering going on down here on this ol' sorry earth. But if you remain unshakable, especially with the likes of Rosie O'Hara, then your faith will prove out when situations seem hopeless. Just keep your faith, and His purpose *will* come to pass, and you *will* see that it will be good."

A sheepish grin turned the corners of Son's mouth upward. He brushed the sand from his hands and held his shoulders back, standing tall and straight. "Yep, you are so right, Katie. The Master is gonna make this ol' sorry world a better place for all us folks, and I'm gonna make sure to walk the right road."

"No turn-abouts!" Katie laughed.

Son cast an astute look towards Rosie, the girl who had made the insolent remarks. Kicking the water, she sent waves rushing onto the sandy shore, washing away the remnants of Son's frog houses. He laid his hand on the cool sand. "Yep, one day, this ol' black boy ain't gonna live in no house of mud and sticks. I am gonna live in a mighty, fine mansion. 'Cause I'm gonna keep my eyes on the road, and no U-turns! And Katie's gonna be right there with me!"

For a while, Son indulged in his thoughts as he dreamed about his future. He felt gratified that he and Katie would always be lifetime friends. He listened as the crickets and cicadas strummed their motors, whirling a symphony through the air.

Suddenly, Son remembered Katie's promise to take him hunting. As he stood, his eyes eagerly searched for his friend. She was almost out of sight as she walked stealthily down the path. Katie never tarried.

"That girl gots squirrel on her mind," he said, laughing. Quickly, he scurried to catch up with his faithful friend, a friend well acquainted with all of his faults and one whom he could trust with his secret dreams.

Son did not hear the sound of crackling twigs and crunching leaves behind him. He was unaware that a malevolent and wicked character had materialized from behind the trees nearby. Like an indolent sloth, the stranger slowly slithered towards the river's edge. For a short while, the imprint of Son's hand remained in the sand. Another imprint remained, an imp's grin on a satanic face—Creel Burr's!

Chapter 3

FULL CIRCLE

The sun beamed hot on Katie's head. Perspiration trickled down her face as she pushed her blond hair from her forehead. One eye closed, she carefully took aim and squeezed the trigger of her Henry rifle. The small gray squirrel perched on the limb of the giant oak fell to the ground.

"Got him, Kat!" yelled Son. "Nobody within ten counties can outshoot you." He threw the lifeless rumple of fur into the brown croaker sack with the others. He opened the sack wide and stared at the bounty of fresh meat. "Yes sirree bobcat! Gonna have mighty fine eatin' tonight. My taste buds are just a jumpin'. Gonna have fried squirrel, grits, and gravy."

Katie fanned herself from the sweltering heat. Cautiously, she reloaded the rifle. The corners of her lips perked up, forming a devilish grin that slowly crept across her face. "Maybe," she said as she winked at Son.

"You always wink at me when you know you're right. Have you ever noticed?"

"Not really." She smiled teasingly. "You know what they say—a wink is as good as a nod."

"Only when you're trying to sell your mules!"

Katie erupted with a gusty laugh. "Okay, Son, point made. Now, since that has been established, let's head for home. It's a long walk, so we'll cut through the woods over to the O'Hara place and then cross the railroad tracks. We can make better time by going that way. Shoot, we might run into that cantankerous ol' heifer, Rosie."

Son, laughing out loud, slapped his thighs as he threw the croaker sack over his shoulder. "Yep, that girl ain't nothin' but a cantankerous ol' heifer! She ain't got the sense God promised a billy goat."

"Don't be too hard on Rosie. She just doesn't have the proper raising that you've had. Give her some slack."

"Whatever you say, Katie." Underneath his breath, Son mumbled, "She's still a cantankerous ol' heifer."

Soon, Katie and Son reached the railroad tracks. Suddenly, Katie stopped, tilted her head, and sniffed the air. The smoke from a nearby campfire burned her nostrils.

"Shhh."

Son nodded. At a snail's pace, Katie and Son crept to the top of the railroad bed. Peering down into the bottom of the ravine, they spied an old hobo sitting by the fire. Intently, they watched as the man stirred the sweltering coals with a stick. Even though hobos rode the rails and made camps along the tracks, few camped on the land that belonged to the McAllisters.

Katie took a deep breath and bravely scrambled down the ridge with Son on her heels. Calmly, she walked up to the stranger, who was unknown to McAllister's land. For a moment, there was a brief silence as she stared into the fire.

Finally, she spoke. "This place is McAllister's farm. Take a rest. Take from the land enough bounty to feed yourself. Take no more. Leave the land the way you found it." She pointed to the campfire. "Make sure you throw some water on your fire before you leave."

This girl is arrogant, thought the old vagrant. However, he knew if he wanted to stay awhile on McAllister's land, he would have to appeal to her good nature. "Pleased to meet ya, Katie."

Startled, Katie wondered how this visitor knew her name. The man extended his hand in a gentlemanly gesture. However, Katie did not respond. Instincts told her that this stranger was not one with whom she should make friendly acquaintance.

The stranger, sensing her uneasiness, ignored Katie's apprehension and boldly stated, "I be Creel Burr. Can't tell you much about myself. Been ridin' the rails for so long, can't remember where I came from and don't rightly know where I'm going."

Katie suspiciously eyed the man named Creel Burr. This rogue of a hobo hosted a craggy and unkempt look. Clothes, soiled and ragged, reeked with an abhorrent stench. Long, tousled gray hair encased an aging face sporting a prominent set of whiskers. A distinctive, toothless grimace transformed into a devious smile. Dull eyes, narrowing to a squint, were characteristic of deceitfulness. Most notable was a faded red bandana tied around his neck.

An iniquitous sneer slowly crept across Creel's face. An icy gaze glared deep into Katie's eyes. "How old are you?" he asked.

Katie's answer, quick and decisive, seemed to bark. "Seventeen. Pretty soon eighteen. Old enough to take care of myself."

Creel eased closer, attempting to lure Katie into his proximity. Proceeding carefully, she shifted the rifle to a ready position.

"You'd better sit tight, Mr. Burr. I just reloaded this Henry, and I can send you to the devil's Hell in about as much time as it would take you to bend over and scratch your nasty behind."

Eyes wide with fear, Son's gaze darted from Katie's face to the rifle she held in her hands. The rigid muscles in his throat tightened. He swallowed hard, almost gulping.

Continuing to ignore the staunch remarks of the girl holding the Henry, Creel went on to inquire, "What ya doin' keepin' company with a coon boy, girl? Don't you know whites don't associate with colored?"

The crude and defenseless reference to Son's color embarrassed the young boy. Shamefully, he shoved his hands in his pockets, scuffed his feet, and bowed his head.

Katie continued to glare at Creel. "Hold your head up, Son," she said. "Being the color you are is nothing to be ashamed of."

She grimaced as she looked hard and long at the offender. "I don't particularly take to your calling my friend a name, sir. The McAllisters never refer to people of color as 'coons,' 'darkies,' or any other derogatory name, Mr. Burr! I was raised with the knowledge that *all* of God's children are made from the same dirt. And may I remind you, skin is only superficial! The Lord doesn't play favorites, Mr. Burr, and in this neck of the woods, no one is more important than the other. Therefore, sir, if you would kindly apologize, my friend and I will take our leave."

Staunch and proud, Katie stood impatiently waiting for an apology from this despicable scoundrel of a man.

The rogue sensed her anger. "Sorry, Katie. I didn't mean to offend."

"Don't forget the campfire," Katie barked as she turned to leave. She trudged up the hill. Eagerly, Son followed.

As Katie and Son neared the top of the hill, Creel yelled from below, "I sure would appreciate it if you would give me one of those squirrels you've got stowed away in that croaker sack!"

Instantly, Katie stopped and whirled around. Reaching inside the sack for a squirrel, she tossed the furry ball below to the ground next to Creel. Quickly, he snatched it up and busily began stripping the skin and fur from the animal. As she turned to go, she did not see the evil, sinister glare in Creel's eyes.

As Katie and Son trekked down the lane, Son frowned. "How did he know that we had squirrels in our sack?"

"How did he know my name?"

Son thought for a moment. Then he answered, "Maybe he was spying on us, and we didn't even know it."

"Seems that way," was Katie's response. She began to wonder about this mysterious stranger. Intuition tugged at her, telling her that Creel Burr was a man one could never trust.

As the two friends trudged down McAllister's Lane, Katie looked out upon barren fields, parched and dry. By this time of the year, the land should have been burgeoning with lush, green crops. Instead, it was a desolate sea of dry dirt. Devastation would be even greater if the rains did not come soon. Looking upwards to the cloudless sky, she bit her bottom lip and whispered a prayer that Creel Burr would act responsibly with his campfire.

Son broke the silence. "When do you think it's going to rain, Katie?"

Katie cast a hard-eyed glance towards Son. "How in a jack rabbit's tail do I know?" She kicked the dirt. The dust filled her nostrils.

Son shuffled the soil around with his foot and began to stutter. "I'm sorry, Kat. I was just asking a question. Didn't mean to make you mad."

A crumpled brow and a softening face showed Katie's concern. She never had talked to Son in such a manner. Kind and gentle was her usual nature. Her voice was now tender. "I'm sorry. I'm just worried that without the rain, we won't be able to put a garden in this year. Because of this dang Depression, we don't have the money to plant, but we sure do need some rain for a garden. Times are already tough, but they will get tougher."

"Don't worry, Kat. You and us Kings will figure out what to do no matter how tough times get. Ma always says that eternal riches are more important than fleeting things of the world."

"Yeah, but those fleeting things of the world won't put food in your stomach."

"But Katie, we got squirrel!"

Katie laughed. Then, in a voice more plaintive, she exclaimed, "We sure do!"

As Katie and Son approached the Kings' weather-beaten small house, they noticed Jezra King, Son's father, sitting on the front steps. Jezra, a black tenant farmer born and raised on this farm, had lived here all of his life with his wife, Sadie, and their only child, Son. Bound to the land, his roots grew deep on this farm he loved.

Many years ago, when the economy began to fail, the majority of black families migrated to other cities, mostly northern. Both white and black had tried desperately to scratch a living from the soil, but desperate times left them with no other choice except to leave the South in hopes of finding better opportunities elsewhere. However, Jezra chose to remain. During these poverty-stricken times, he was not paid wages. Instead, to compensate, he was given a garden spot and free housing. Included was use of any facilities and farming implements.

Besides, all that a man could eat was right here on McAllister's land. Emerald pastures and forest-clad hills abounded with wild game. White-tailed deer and wild turkeys flecked the hills and swamps, not to mention a bounty of squirrels and rabbits. Lazy streams and the river nearby teamed with bream, catfish, and trout. Everything needed to feed his family was here. Jezra never even gave it a thought to leave this place and live somewhere else.

The farm on which the Kings lived was settled generations ago by the McAllisters, part of a small group of early pioneers who settled in this wire grass region. Migrating from Tennessee, the McAllisters, the pillars of this parcel of land, nestled deep within the heart of Southwest Georgia. Eventually, small, sleepy communities evolved in the surrounding area. But this piece of land was their home. They called it McAllister's Lane.

In recent years, Katie's grandparents had passed away. Because her mother had died giving birth, Katie was the only child born to Ann and Thomas McAllister. There on McAllister's Lane, she lived contentedly with her father, Thomas, at least until this year, 1933.

Thomas McAllister, like many of the other farmers in the area, was riding the rails east to west, north to south, jumping off trains at any town, hoping to find employment of any kind. Katie had received letters from every little 'pothole town' from Monroe, Louisiana, to Montgomery, Alabama. The last letter received from her father was postmarked from the largest town near McAllister's Lane—Albany, Georgia. Gradually, Thomas was easing his way back home and to his only child. In the meantime, Katie remained living alone in their home at the end of McAllister's Lane. She felt safe and secure in knowing that the Kings' home was at the first bend, only a holler away.

Jezra smiled as he cast an approving glance towards Katie and then to Son. He knew that the two friends had grown up working and playing together on the farm, trotting every rabbit trail and blazing new paths over every inch of this land.

Jezra asked, "Where you two young'uns been off to?"

Son beamed. "Me and Katie been huntin'. Got some squirrels for supper, Pa!"

"Well, get to cleaning 'em. Sadie and Mrs. O'Hara are in the kitchen talking about some recipe for some kind of relish. At least I think that's what they're talking about!" He chuckled.

Son blurted, "Pa, I gotta get back to the sloughs. I left my catfish poles set. Gotta check my hooks. You know, Pa, you always say nary should go to waste."

Katie laughed. "And we for sure don't want to waste!" She glanced at Son and said, "Go check your poles. I'll stay here and help Sadie clean the squirrels."

Son grabbed a lantern to light his way in case he got caught by dusk. Then he scampered off to check his lines, stopping only momentarily to shout over his shoulder, "Thanks, Katie! I owe you one!"

Jezra said, "Grass sho' don't grow under that boy's feet!"

In the kitchen, Sadie and Mrs. O'Hara were sitting at the eating table, the place central to the Kings' family life, laughing and joking as these two friends often did. Katie smiled. Bigotry! Not a practice applied here. Two women, one white and the other black, had never allowed the color of their skin to cause this circle of friendship to be defiled. The King house was a God-fearing place where peace was sought instead of confrontation. Adversity was meaningless within this family that based its morals upon truth, forgiveness, and humility.

"Katie!" exclaimed Sadie when she looked up and saw the young woman walking towards her. "How's my baby?"

Because Sadie worked in the McAllisters' home, she had cared for Katie from early infancy. Each and every day, her heart would melt a little more as she rocked and held the motherless baby in her arms. The first time Katie's soft, tiny fingers wrapped around Sadie's, a strong love was bonded—never to be broken!

Sadie smiled at the girl with hair like corn silk and eyes as blue as forget-me-nots, the young girl who was on the brink of becoming a woman. "What ya got in that sack, girl?"

"Squirrels for supper!" Katie boasted as she rummaged through the kitchen with a sudden and inexplicable urge to gorge on peas plucked from Sadie's garden that afternoon.

Mrs. O'Hara interrupted. "Where is Rosie? Wasn't she with you and Son earlier today at the river?"

"Yes, ma'am. We left her there playing in the water. She's not home yet."

"No, not yet."

Mrs. O'Hara's crumpled brow showed concern. It was unusual for Rosie to stay at the river by herself for a long period of time. She continued, "Well, Sadie, better get going and see if that child is home yet. If she's not there, she's got a whoopin' coming her way!"

Mrs. O'Hara stood, straightened her dress, and cheerfully said her farewells. "See you girls later. Save me that recipe, Sadie." And she was gone!

Sadie's eyes gleamed, not only because she enjoyed fresh meat on her table, but mostly because she loved the young woman standing before her. "Come on, girl. Let's start cleaning them critters you got in that sack. Fried squirrels and gravy on Jezra's plate is gonna make him mighty happy. He's gettin' pretty tired of catfish stew!"

"Sadie, do you think that you and Mrs. O'Hara will always be friends?" inquired Katie.

The soft-spoken Sadie gently put her arms around the white child she had raised and nurtured. "Always. Friendships may be tried and tested, but they always last."

Katie smiled at Sadie, who was always true to herself when it came to imparting authentic wisdom. Through the years, Sadie helped her understand that true friendships did last when tried and tested. When friendship is *tried*, hate and bitterness are overshadowed by love and forgiveness; when *tested*, it has the power to break the chains of prejudice and the shackles of racism.

As Katie thought about the true meaning of friendship, she wondered if the mysterious stranger, Creel Bur, had ever had a friend. Suspicion and distrust left a lingering feeling that instead of meeting a meek and kind-hearted man, she had just had an encounter with evil!

As Katie reminisced, the day's events seemed to have traveled full circle. From love and friendship to evil and death, then returning to hearts filled with love and friendship.

Katie glanced through the window and saw a lone chicken hawk flying away with a baby chick chirping in distress. The mother hen, busily scratching the ground for bugs, never noticed that the bird of prey had zoomed down from the sky and with his sharp claws had silently scooped her baby away.

Chapter 4

ABOVE THE LAW

An old spiritual filled the air as Son loudly sang:

"O never you mind what Satan say,

Going home in the chariot in the morning.

Judgment is coming every day,

Going home in the chariot in the morning."

Son carefully unhooked one catfish, then two as he hauled in his catch. A pole set in the early part of the day was bent with the weight of another wiggling fish.

"O sinner man, you better pray. Going home in the..." As Son backed from the river's edge, pulling in his heavy catch, he tripped over something in the thick underbrush. Looking around, he wondered what had caused him to fall backwards. Maybe a fallen limb from one of the big live oaks was the culprit. Then, suddenly, he spied the unimaginable! The reason was clear. Son had tripped over legs! Legs not belonging to an animal but a human!

Momentarily, he froze, not certain what to do. Frightened, he hurriedly retrieved his lantern. Just as quickly, he scurried back to the body, which was pulled into the bush, leaving only legs partially exposed. Frantically, Son held the light high to view the half-hidden corpse. He gasped. It was Rosie! Rosie O'Hara!

"Rosie!" Son screamed. "Good Lord, what has happened to you? Rosie, get up!"

There was only silence, no movement. Son attempted to rouse his friend but soon realized that Rosie was not going to get up. Not ever! Her body was cold and rigid. Her neck was swollen and had red marks. Someone had strangled Rosie!

A tightening throat caused Son to struggle, refraining from a scream, especially, after noticing that Rosie's body was bruised, bloody and naked.

"Oh, Rosie, what has someone gone and done to you?" Slowly, Son pulled off his jacket and gently covered Rosie's frail, cold body as he sniffed and wiped away trickling tears. "What is your poor mama gonna do without you?"

As he pushed her reddish-blond hair away from her face, Son noticed that the culprit, whoever he might be, had not only taken Rosie's ribbon but had cut off a lock of her hair.

"Where is your ribbon, girl?" Son cried as he felt around the ground for it. "You always wore that blue ribbon. It looked so pretty in your hair." He affectionately patted her cold arm.

Feeling nauseous and distressed, Son suddenly looked up and saw men carrying lanterns and long staffs steadily moving in his direction. Beating the underbrush, they loudly called out, "Rosie!"

The eerie sound of the baying of hounds frightened the young boy. Quickly, he scampered to his feet and gazed down at the still body of Rosie O'Hara.

"They're gonna think that I did this!" The situation appeared dire. Son had no alternative, he thought, but to run for his life.

It seemed like hours for Katie, Sadie, and Jezra as they anxiously waited for Son to return. Although worried, the consensus was that Son was having a good night of fishing. Finally, Katie decided to walk home and started her trek down the lazy, winding lane. The sky, illuminated by the light of the moon, was star-filled. The breeze was fair, and the trees gently swayed. Katie's spirits were high as she strolled to her house at the end of McAllister's Lane.

Suddenly, in the distance, Katie could hear the sound of barking dogs and men loudly conversing. In her heart was a voice telling her that dark trouble was ahead. Slowly and more closely now through the shadowy night, she could see a zealous and ruthless crowd carrying torches and moving in her direction.

Something or someone was being tugged behind them. A closer look revealed who it was. It was Son! A rope was tied around Son! The irate mob was dragging him, kicking and screaming, to the O'Haras' farm. Desperate and afraid, Son struggled to resist the tug on the rope as he wailed in distress.

Heart racing, Katie sprinted towards the clamor to confront the horde of angry men. Mr. O'Hara was among the group. Hysterical, Katie ran straight to Rosie's father.

"What are you doing?" she screamed. "Why do you have a rope tied around Son's neck?"

Mr. O'Hara, seemingly in a daze, continued to walk and stared straight ahead, ignoring Katie's presence.

Within a brief time, the demented group passed the Kings' home. Sadie and Jezra dashed out of their house.

"What's going on here?" yelled Jezra. "Why you got my boy?"

Sadie, too, hastened to Son. Desperately, she tried to pull the rope from around his neck. One man whom she did not recognize knocked her to the ground.

Without breaking his stride, Jezra reached for a staff carved out of an oak limb leaning against a post. Valiantly, he fought his way to Sadie, swinging the staff around his head, hitting one of the assailants. A loud thud sounded, propelling a man facedown, prone, and eliciting a painful moan. Someone from behind sent a crashing blow against Jezra's back, causing him to stagger and fall to his knees. Someone else hit him with the butt of his gun. Stunned, Jezra fell next to his bewildered and frightened wife.

The evil pack reached the O'Haras' home at the end of McAllister's Lane. There, the men tied Son's hands behind his back and hoisted him on the back of a wagon. The wagon was driven underneath a lone, isolated tree known in the community as the Judgment Tree.

Katie's heart pounded as she recalled stories from the past about the Judgment Tree. Living in the backwoods of South Georgia, people made their own justice. Anyone committing a heinous crime, whether stranger or kin, fell to his or her demise at the hands of a quickly assembled judge and jury. Conviction was made the backwoods way—hastily and with bias. It was called the backwoods law!

Effortlessly, Jezra, who had by now regained his strength and balance, sprinted down the lane and fought his way through to his son. Sadie was close behind. Brutal men continuously knocked him down. He stumbled to his knees and lay motionless on the ground.

Sadie ran from one incensed man to the next, begging and pleading for mercy on her son's life. With all her might, she pushed her way through the crowd to Mrs. O'Hara. "What is going on? Why are they doing this?"

Mrs. O'Hara stared at the woman whom she had once called friend. Only a few hours before, they were sitting together at a kitchen table, laughing and talking about a recipe for relish. Now Mrs. O'Hara's eyes narrowed with hatred.

"Your boy raped and killed my Rosie!" she screamed. "For that, I curse you!"

Sadie cried out with pain that only a mother in sorrow could understand. "No, no! Not my boy! How can you say such awful things?"

"They say they found Son's jacket lying across Rosie's body! They saw him running away!"

Between sobs, Sadie screamed, "No! Stop them! Just because he ran doesn't mean he is guilty!" She shook Mrs. O'Hara's arm vehemently. "Wouldn't you run if you were a black boy and were found next to a white girl's body? Please, give him a chance to speak. I beg you, let him explain."

Mrs. O'Hara remained unyielding. Cold eyes stared ahead, glaring. A rope was thrown over the limb of the big tree. A hangman's noose was slipped over Son's neck.

Frantically, the boy cried out for Sadie and Jezra. Desperate, frightened eyes searched for Katie. "Katie!" he yelled. "What did I do wrong?" he cried, choking. "Katie! I didn't take the wrong road! No turn about! Help me!" he begged.

Katie grabbed a neighbor, one of the assailants, by his arm. With all of her strength, she forcibly turned the man towards her. Her heart raced as she yelled out, "You are making a terrible mistake! You know Son could never have done anything like this!"

The supposed friend with cold, dark eyes did not reply. Turning her attention to Mr. O'Hara, Katie's pleas fell upon deaf ears. The sound of her voice was not heard over the shouting of the loud, angry, murderous mob.

Pushing her way through the incensed crowd, Katie lunged at another friend and neighbor. "You have to stop this! I beg you! What you are doing is above the law!"

The irate man dragged Katie to another wagon parked nearby. Even as he tied her to one of the wheels by her wrists, she fought valiantly. With every ounce of strength, she would not surrender. With as much might as she could muster, she kicked and scratched. Her hard teeth penetrated the assailant's hand. The capturer struck her across the jaw causing her to loose consciousness. No one interceded. No one came to her rescue.

Standing impassively next to the wagon was Rosie's mother. Stern, callous eyes stared at the accused black boy. Someone from the crowd handed Mrs. O'Hara a whip. Slowly and deliberately, she walked up to the mules harnessed to the wagon. Emotionless, she glared at Son. Within that same moment, she cast the stinging leather across the rump of the mule. The mule jerked, causing the team to explode into a dead run down the lane. Dangling from the Judgment Tree, Son frantically squirmed, kicking his feet as he struggled to breathe.

Sadie sprinted to the aid of her only child. With all of her strength, she desperately tried to hold him up by his legs, straining to push him upward to prevent him from choking. She stood shaking and unrelenting, holding the weight of her child up with her arms and shoulders; her body quivered under the undue strain.

Silently, the crowd watched. Finally, someone whispered, "Why doesn't she go ahead and let go? Let the boy die."

Slowly, Jezra, now on his feet, inched his way towards Sadie. He reached for her tightly grasped hands, pulling them from around Son's legs. Sadie fell in a heap upon the ground. Jezra, realizing that his boy's death was imminent, yanked downward on Son's legs, breaking his neck and ensuring a quick and merciful death. Jezra trembled. His heart ached as he knelt beside the sobbing mother of his only child.

The sound of Sadie's wailing pelted Katie's eardrums and roused her from unconsciousness. Staggering, she pulled herself up by the rope. Vigilantly, she scanned the crowd, studying the face of every man there—neighbors and, she thought, friends. Among the crowd were also men she did not recognize.

Standing on the back of a wagon was a stranger, cursing and shouting orders as he stirred the men to anger. Although in control, he stood in awe of the situation as emotionless, cold eyes scanned the crowd. Just as dark and dreary was his attire. Dressed in black Western wear, with a shoestring necktie, or bolo, hanging around his neck, he seemed almost satanic.

Katie's eyes were drawn to the reflection of the silver bolo slide as it shone brightly in the light of the torches. She would never forget him or the others. Methodically, she etched their faces in her mind. With strength and courage, she yelled. The now-subdued men turned towards her. Her voice was scratchy but clear. "I will never forget your faces and the evil you have done!" Wide-eyed, her gaze darted from one to the other as she continued to blast away. "Upon each of you I will seek my revenge! Watch and wait for your day of reckoning when all of you will answer to *me* for what you have done. You *will* stand accountable!"

Among the mob was a few of Katie's neighbors. Besides Rosie's parents, there were the McKinnons, Whiskey Jones, Buster Reese and Jackson Buford. They well knew of her reputation of being a sharp shooter with a Henry rifle. Those men shivered for they knew that one day, Katie's wrath would definitely descend upon each and every one of them.

As for the others, the strangers, simply mocked her as they cheered. The stranger who tied her to the wagon, slapped her again across her face. He barked, "And, what are you going to do, nigger lover?"

Suddenly, Katie shivered as she caught a glimpse of a familiar man standing aloof from the crowd. His evil eyes danced, and a grimacing, toothless face cast an eerie smile. Tied around his neck was a faded red bandana. Wiping away tears, she locked eyes with Creel Burr. She whispered, "As for you, Creel Burr, you will be the first I send to Satan's hell!"

As dawn neared, the crowd had dispersed. Sadie, Jezra, and Katie were the only ones who remained at the Judgment Tree. All night, they had knelt beside the lifeless body of Son King. They held onto each other tightly, weeping uncontrollably and praying for consolation.

Katie helped Jezra load Son's body into the back of Jezra's wagon. Her friend would no longer reside in a stick house, as Rosie had taunted, but a new home that would be a mansion. Katie's endless promise came to mind—he would never walk alone.

As they drove down the lane to the family cemetery, Katie rubbed her red, swollen wrists. The hooves of the mules clonked, and the wagon creaked. As Katie stared down the lane that stretched out before them, hatred filled her vulnerable heart. Forgiveness was not an option.

"All in due time," she whispered. "I'll get them. They will pay with their lives…even if I have to give mine!"

Jezra's strong, masculine voice ordered the mules to halt with a commanding, "Whoa!"

They had arrived at the cemetery, Son's final resting place. Sadie sat stoically staring at the ground as the grave was dug. There was no casket, no vault—only a wool blanket to wrap Son's body. Sadie sat silently. Her heart sank. Her gaze was fixed and red; her swollen eyes never blinked.

When the burial was over, Sadie remained at the gravesite. Jezra motioned for Katie to walk with him to the wagon. He began, "Sadie and me talked when you left to go get the wagon. We're going to leave McAllister's Lane."

"But why?" questioned Katie. "Don't leave me here alone. This farm is your home, too. Together we'll beat this."

Jezra and Katie were unaware that Sadie had quietly walked up from behind. Before anyone could speak, she blurted out, her tone cold and unyielding, "This is not my home anymore. Not after last night." Sadie grasped her apron and began to cry uncontrollably. "I can't stay in a place where there is so much hate. I can't stay in a place that reminds me of what happened to our boy."

Katie clasped Sadie's arm tightly as she pleaded, "They will pay for hanging Son. I will see to it. Please, don't leave. What will I do here all alone?"

Sadie and Jezra knew they were doing the right thing by leaving. There would be no peace here, only heartbreak and hatred. Remaining here would only lead to more confrontation and complications. For them, there was no other option but to leave McAllister's Lane. And Sadie must leave her beloved Katie.

"You don't understand," Sadie exclaimed as she buried her head in her hands and sobbed. "I just watched my husband lay our only child in a cold, dark hole."

The sadness was overwhelming. Katie's heart, galled by unbearable sorrow, was breaking with this yoke of remorse. In the middle of McAllister's Lane, once her place of refuge, she cried from the depths of her heart and soul.

Reluctantly, Katie murmured, "I understand." She held onto Sadie as both cried vehemently. Sobbing, she asked Jezra, "Where will you go?"

"I'm not sure. Maybe we'll just get in our boat and let it take us down river 'til we come to the first place that feels safe."

"Albany is down river. That's where Papa is. Will you stop there, Jezra, and find Papa?"

"We'll see, Katie. First things come first. Get Sadie away from this place first and then find your papa."

Hot, stinging tears streamed down Katie's cheeks. Discouraged and defeated, she managed to murmur, "When will you leave?"

"Tomorrow. Today, I have some unfinished business, and I need your help."

"I'll do anything you ask."

Jezra watched his wife as she slowly strolled back to the grave site. Sadly, they watched as Sadie laid across the freshly dug grave. Gently, she padded and kissed the soil where her only child laid just a few feet below.

"Right now, I'm going to take Sadie home to pack a few things. As soon as she is okay to leave, I'll come back and tell you my plans."

Katie grabbed Jezra's shirt sleeve. "This was once a happy place. But now, it'll never be the same. I want to go with you cause I can't live here anymore either."

"No, Katie. You have to stay. Don't you know, girl, that we have different skins. What do you think will happen to me and Sadie if a white girl is caught with us?"

He turned to go, stopped, and dropped his head, feeling compelled to succumb to the adversity that was knocking at his door. "You've got to be strong, Katie, so I can be strong for Sadie. You know how she feels about you. She loves you like you are her baby." He paused. "When tomorrow comes, you can take us down the river in the boat. After we get to where we think we need to be, you got to come back home. We'll do it that way so it won't be so hard on Sadie. Understand, girl?"

As Katie wiped the tears, she relunctanly replied, "Okay. I'll do what you say. But only for Sadie's sake. But, Jezra. I can promise you that there will be a time of reckoning. I will sit and watch and wait. When the time and place is right, I will deal with each and everyone of them."

"Please, Katie," begged Jezra, "don't let bitterness and hate gain a foothold in your life. For Sadie's sake, will you promise me that? And tomorrow, when you leave us, don't cry so Sadie will know that you are gonna be okay."

Glaring up towards the sky, Katie caught sight of an eagle sailing on the currents of the wind and soaring to the heights above. Suddenly, a strong and serene calm filled her broken heart. The lone soaring eagle flapped its wings, taking it to greater heights. She wiped the tears away. "No more, tears, Jezra. Only payback!"

Chapter 5

IN THE MIDST OF STRANGERS

$\mathcal{I}$n the quiet of the day, Katie and Jezra worked incessantly, filling the wagon with any flammable materials they could find. They loaded every available resource from cow dung to rotten limbs and dried boards.

Word was sent out to neighboring communities about the events of the previous night and what was to transpire this very night. Swift runners and word of mouth sufficed as the only means of communication, the result of isolation coupled with lack of telephones and electricity.

Soon, a sultry darkness approached, filling the night with eeriness. Katie and Jezra drove the wagon to a lone tree that had stood isolated on the O'Haras' farm for generations. Standing aloft, the Judgment Tree stood as a symbol of lawlessness and injustice.

No sooner had Katie and Jezra arrived than every black man and boy old enough to hoist a limb or use a crosscut saw began to appear. Silently, they worked all through the night under the quiet of the stars. Limbs were cut, sawed, and piled around the base of the tree, leaving a five-foot stump exposed as a reminder of narrow-minded intolerance. Kindling and other flammables brought in on wagons were heavily doused with kerosene and piled on top of the limbs.

Slowly and deliberately, Jezra struck a match. Emotionless, he stood watching it fizzle, then burn. He cast the burning match onto the kerosene-soaked pile, causing a huge flame to ignite. The fire roared. Soon, the Judgment Tree was engulfed in flames. It became a raging inferno. No longer did it stand as the emblem of hatred and abomination. No longer did it serve as a symbol of oppression and injustice, but rather as an icon of liberty, peace, and hope.

Sitting on the porch from his house atop the hill and across the meadow was Mr. O'Hara. Stoically, he sat all night, rocking and watching below as the men quietly worked. His wife, wrapped in a shawl to break the chill, soon joined her husband. No words were exchanged.

The stench of the burning timber stung their nostrils. The sound of the crackling wood pelted the O'Haras' eardrums. As the flames roared and reached up towards the heavens, sparks danced in the darkness. The couple rocked and watched.

Hate grew the tree, thought Mr. O'Hara, *and courage burned it down.*

The people who came to Jezra's aid remained until the Judgment Tree was a pile of smoldering ashes, leaving only a charred post of the trunk. Intentionally left, it stood like a monument. Out of the ashes, it stood as powerful symbol of freedom.

Decades ago, their families had walked in darkness, held in bondage in the South. They understood that to be truly free, a life of freedom comes only from their faith in the living God.

Regardless of race, freedom came from living a life based on His divine power. Liberation did not set one free. Bondage did not keep one held in captivity. To walk out of darkness, one had to first walk in the light of Jesus Christ.

As quietly as they came, they left, slipping away before the morning sun aroused curious and perhaps malevolent opponents. At the break of dawn, a new day approached; so did a new spirit of hope.

At the river's edge, Sadie patiently waited. The johnboat, filled with meager possessions, would safely carry her, Jezra, and Katie downriver, hopefully to a place where new beginnings, new possibilities, and true hope could be envisioned.

As soon as Katie and Jezra arrived, Katie jumped in the front of the boat. Carefully, she laid her shotgun under the bow along with her long coat, a hat, and some jerky. With a mighty heave, Jezra pushed the john out into the gentle, flowing waters of the Flint—into a journey they would not soon forget! "What took you so long?" asked Sadie. "I've been waiting here since early morning."

"Nothing for you to worry about," began Jezra. "Me and Katie had to turn the livestock out of the corrals. Better for them to water at the streams and eat on the land than go hungry waiting for Katie to get home. Now, settled back, woman. Like I said, ain't nothing for you to worry about."

In the beginning, the cool, grayish water flowed slowly and tenuously like soft winds on a spring day. However, miles down the river, the sky very quickly darkened as a thunderstorm approached. Lightning popped, illuminating the sky. Thunder roared. A hard rain and violent wind fiercely pounded the small boat as the storm raged. The slow-moving Flint, once calm and complacent, became increasingly rapid. Katie held her breath as she and Jezra fought to hold the boat steady as the waters rushed around ominous rocks protruding from the water.

Jezra shouted, "Katie! I see a slough up ahead. Let's try to make it there before we crash and overturn."

The slough was a good place to wait out the rain. There, the water away from the currents was much calmer. The gigantic trees that gently bowed from the banks made an excellent shelter. Spanish moss hanging from the low limbs provided a break from the gusty winds. Once the boat was secured, they patiently waited until the storm calmed. Hours later, the wind and rain subsided, and the troubled waters ceased, leaving a tranquil peace.

"Think we can go now, Jezra?" asked Katie.

"I think so."

Jezra stood up to push against one of the trees with his paddle. Unaware that a brown water snake was hanging on an overhead limb, he accidentally struck the reptile, causing it to fall into the boat. The snake fell in Sadie's lap and then landed in the bottom of the boat near her feet. She screamed.

Without hesitation, Jezra quickly snatched up the snake, hurling it into the water, but not before it staunchly bit him on the hand! Although not poisonous, the snake's bite was painful.

Jezra moaned, "Dang it! Didn't see that coming."

Promptly, Sadie tore a piece of cloth from her underslip and wrapped Jezra's hand. "Oh, Jezra, when is the Lord gonna stop punishing us? Is it because we're cursed?"

"Cursed? What do you mean?"

"Because our skin is black, our race is marked, and bad things happen to us."

Tenderly, Jezra cupped his wife's face in his hands. "First of all, God is not punishing us, Sadie."

"But He took our boy."

"Sadie, my sweet wife, God is holy, and He don't have no favorites. Don't matter if you are rich or poor, black or white, He is righteous and holy across all lines." Tenderly, he kissed his beloved Sadie on her forehead. "Now, woman, you get all them thoughts out of your head."

Pulling her close, Jezra silently prayed that his comforting words would be sufficient for every heartache, burden, and sorrow his dear wife was experiencing.

"Let's go," he said. "Let's get on downriver and find us a new home."

Although Katie watched with admiration and respect, she was saddened that Sadie was anxiously looking forward to starting over away from McAllister's Lane. Her gut wrenched, but she remained silent.

Downriver, Sadie said, "Jezra, you got to find me a place to relieve myself. I've been holding my water for way too long."

Often the river would wind and twist, and occasionally the banks sloped into an easy incline of rock and clay, and often a sandbar. Luckily, Jezra spotted such a landing. He shouted, "Kat, there's a sandbar up ahead! Let's land there for a while. Sadie needs to go, and I need to rest."

Katie willingly obeyed. As they reached the sandbar, they pulled the boat up on the wet sand. Sadie sprinted for a tree. Jezra sat down on the sand. Slowly, he rocked back and forth, holding his aching hand.

"Is it hurting, Jezra?"

"Hurts bad, Katie. Hurts bad," Jezra moaned. "But don't tell Sadie. She has too much on her mind to worry 'bout me."

Katie winked. Suddenly, she burst into laughter.

"What's so funny, girl?"

"I was just remembering that I told Son a wink was as good as a nod. Son said, 'Only if I'm selling mules.'"

"Yeah, that boy sure had a way 'bout him." Jezra suddenly became overwhelmed with grief that cut straight to his heart.

"I'm sorry. I didn't mean to get you upset," pleaded Katie.

"I'll be okay. I think that all I need is a little sleep. What you think about Jezra laying his ol' weary bones on this sandbar and taking me a snooze?"

"I think that I agree. It seems like ages since ..." Katie stopped. "Yeah, let's all take a nap."

Soon, the three traveling companions were sleeping soundly on the cool, wet sand. They had hardly slept an hour when Sadie let out a bloodcurdling scream.

"Jezra!"

Jezra and Katie promptly sat up. "What's wrong?"

Sadie pointed. Running off in the bush with a sack of their supplies was a boy about sixteen years of age.

Jezra jumped up. "I'll get him! I'll catch his li'l ol' scrawny butt!"

"No!" Sadie yelled. "Let him go."

"That's our food in that sack, Sadie!"

"And that boy might be hungry. And he might be a needin' that food more than you and me."

Jezra looked at Sadie and then at Katie. He didn't understand. "Sadie?"

"No, Jezra! That could be somebody's boy. Wouldn't you want somebody to feed our boy if he was hungry?"

"Help me get Sadie in the boat, Katie. We need to be going."

No one spoke until they were arrived at the Albany train trestle.

"Oh, my good Lord," said Jezra. "What have we done got ourselves into?"

Katie was aghast, as were the Kings. Never had they seen such an array of poverty! Underneath the train trusses and up on the hill were acres upon acres of throw-together shelters and makeshift homes crudely constructed of anything from strips of canvas to tar paper. The fortunate found abode in lean-tos built against the trees.

Lean bodies indicated that these forsaken people were literally starving. Some people were setting out trotlines with hopes that a good night of fishing would fill empty stomachs in the morning.

Clothes were tattered and worn. Faces were dirty. Hair was unkempt and shaggy. Dejected, children were not playing innocent games. Occasionally, a baby would cry, clinging tenaciously to desolate mothers.

Segregated and discriminated against, the inhabitants of the Negro race lived hopelessly without any expectations of a better life.

Sadie was stunned, but she managed to ask, "Jezra, what are we going to do?"

"We've come too far to turn back."

Jezra got out of the boat and pulled it up onto the shore. Quickly, he turned to Katie. "Get out of the boat on your own. I can't be seen giving you my hand."

"Okay," she replied as she turned to help Sadie.

"No, girl! You can't give her your hand, Katie. We ain't on McAllister's Lane anymore." He turned and gently motioned towards the crowd that watched and waited. "They are watching every move we make. Just one wrong move and they'll be on us like stink on a hog."

He turned to Katie. "I'm going up the hill to talk to someone. Stay here with Sadie."

Willingly, Katie obeyed.

Within a few minutes, Jezra returned. "Katie, it'll soon be dark, and you can't stay here tonight."

"No!" said Sadie. "Katie stays with us!"

Jezra took Sadie by her shoulders. "Listen to me, woman. This ain't McAllister's Lane. These people blame the whites, and whites blame blacks. No white girl can stay here with us. It's not safe! Understand?"

Sadie nodded, even though she did not understand. Her heart ached. More than ever, she needed courage and strength. She realized that her road would be long and filled with distracting obstacles. As for now, she felt discouraged and defeated.

Jezra explained, "The man I talked with told me that another shantytown was on down the river a piece, under the Broad Street bridge. He said white people stayed there."

Jezra and Sadie yearned to put their arms around their beloved Katie but were afraid to do so. Curious eyes were watching!

"Get on down there, Katie, before it gets dark," ordered Jezra. "Sleep there tonight. Then come morning, you hightail it back to McAllister's Lane."

"But, why Jezra? Why can't I stay near you and Sadie?"

"Katie, look around you, girl. Look at the way those people are looking at you. It's not safe here. And, it's not gonna be safe at that other shantytown. When folks are afraid and hungry, Katie, they get dangerous. Now, we talked about this. Remember? You promised me that you would go back home. For Sadie's sake. No one will hurt you there."

"Okay. I'll do what you say. But what about finding my papa? I need him to come home, Jezra. I need him now!"

"I'll find him if I have to walk down every street in this town. If I have to turn every brick upside down, I'll find him. And when I do, I'll send him home to you. That's a promise you can bank on."

Katie glanced over at the sad but angry faces that were staring at her. "Okay, I'll go." She started to reach for Sadie, but hesitated. "You'll always be in my heart. I'll always love you. And I'll be waiting for you to come home."

Tears welled in Sadie's sad eyes. "Maybe. One day. I love you, too." Feeling helpless, Sadie watched her beloved Katie paddle down the river to the Broad Street bridge.

As Katie neared the landing, night was approaching. Under the bridge near the river's edge, she saw several campfires in the distant darkness. The reflection of a fog moon shone on the soft ripples of the water. A cool breeze blowing off the water stung her face. The chill of the night caused her to shiver. She felt overwhelming loneliness on this cold and silent night.

Katie paddled up to a bank where she decided to sleep in the johnboat. Trembling, she wrapped herself in a blanket, moaned, and gently rocked back and forth. Heartrending tears welled in her eyes.

Through chattering teeth, she pleaded, "Please, Lord, I know that I have a heart full of hatred, and I am so angry right now, but I need Papa. Please help Jezra find him." She whispered, "When you come home, Papa, we'll live off the land and never go into town or leave the farm and never see any of those evil, murdering men again. We'll sit on the porch in the evening and listen to the meadowlarks sing their sweet songs and the bobwhites call for their mates. We'll listen to the katydids and watch the fireflies blink."

Katie realized that it would take a power she did not have to overcome this trial. After a silent prayer, she added, "With God's grace, I will be strong again. I will learn to rid my heart of this sadness and be whole. I will learn to forgive, and Father, please heal this nation and these hurting people." Finally, curled into a fetal position in the bottom of the boat, she fell asleep, weary and exhausted.

As the dawn broke, a bleak and dreary sky paved the way for yet another shantytown. Not any different from the black shantytown, this gathering was a maze of sad, forsaken people succumbing to their fate. This place, occupied by whites only, was a continuation of the array of poverty, devastation, and sadness inflicted upon this nation's people.

Stretched before Katie was the result of a mass migration of people from different walks of life. They were ordinary people who had lost their homes. Their life's work had crumbled beneath them. Some were farmers. Others were businessmen, factory workers, lay workers, and even bankers. Jobless and evicted, they had no place to call home. They were part of a nation that felt disgraced. Spirits were broken. Hearts were heavy.

Katie's eyes were drawn to the people who had succumbed to their fate, just like the people under the other train trestle. It was hard for her to comprehend the rationale behind the intensity of these times. More puzzling was the fact that both races shared the same hurt and pain. Both were homeless, helpless, and hopeless. The only difference was the color of their skin, yet they remained segregated within their lives and their hardships.

As Katie slowly walked among the people, she noticed that no one laughed or talked. She spied an old woman attempting to sleep, alone and shivering under a cardboard box. With heart-felt compassion, Katie quietly pulled off her own blanket and wrapped it around the lady's shoulders. Deeply sorrowful and depressed, the young woman's spirits were low. Gradually, she strolled back to her boat, tied to a tree at the river's edge.

Unexpectedly, a small, frail child about ten years of age tugged on Katie's britches. "Ma'am," he began, "is your name Katie McAllister?"

Katie responded, "Yes."

"This ol' man asked me to give this to you." The little boy stretched out his hand, which tightly held a faded red bandana tied neatly in a knot. The boy continued, "He said that he left you a message tied up inside."

With shaking hands, Katie untied the knot. Inside was a blue hair ribbon that she immediately recognized. It belonged to Rosie! Rosie O'Hara!

Katie's stomach churned and knotted. She swallowed hard. Her throat ached as she desperately tried to refrain from screaming. Nervously, she scanned her surroundings.

"Where is he?" she asked the young boy. Her eyes frantically searched for the malevolent man. She repeated, "Where is he?"

The stunned boy's eyes widened when Katie yelled, "Where is he? Where is he, I say?" The frightened boy stammered, "He ... he said that you would find him, ma'am. He said

you would know where to look."

Katie regained her composure. "I'm sorry, boy. I didn't mean to scare you. I just need to find this man. Do you have any idea where he went?"

"No ma'am. Ol' hobos don't hang out here. Usually they hang out under the trestle across the river from the black shantytown with other hobos."

Katie tousled the small child's hair. "What is your name?"

"They call me Root."

"Root? That's an odd name."

"Yeah. I think they call me Root because I'm always rooting around looking for something to eat."

"Are you hungry?"

"I'm always hungry, ma'am."

Katie retrieved a sack from the boat. "Here's some jerky," she said. "Do you need some for your family?"

Root eagerly took the jerky. It didn't take him long before he was gnawing at the tough strips of meat. "Don't have none, ma'am. Ma and Pa died with the fever awhile back."

"I'm so sorry. Who looks after you?"

"I pretty much look after myself, ma'am."

"Root, tell you what. There is plenty of jerky in my pack. You can stay here and eat all you want if you look after my boat until I get back."

A full mouth impaired Root from speaking. Instead, he pointed in the direction where the hobos slept.

A thunderstorm was approaching. Katie grabbed her long sack coat, hat, and her papa's Fox double barrel shotgun concealed inside the john boat. She cast a discerning look towards the darkening sky. "Well, Root, I'd better be going. It looks like rain. Take care of yourself."

As Katie turned to walk away, she glanced back at the young boy, who was busily eating jerky as if it were his last meal. She smiled. "Don't let anybody steal my boat, okay?"

"No ma'am!"

Steadily, Katie walked in the direction of the trestle across from the black shantytown—towards Creel Burr. "I'm coming after you, Creel." Hatred filled her heart; strife filled her soul. "I *will* make you pay. Today is the day that you *will* stand accountable!"

Chapter 6

RESOLVED

*J*t was beginning to drizzle. Katie put on her long coat that hung to the ground and neatly tucked her hair underneath a wide-brim hat. She checked to be sure that her father's Fox double barrel shotgun was concealed underneath the coat. There were two extra shells inside her pocket. Biting her lip, she glanced up at the darkening sky as thunderclouds approached. An overwhelming feeling of loneliness on this cool and silent morning was evident.

Quickly, Katie walked to the trestle, scattering the leaves and trampling the grass under measured and heavy steps. The walk gave her an opportunity to think. Was she making an error in judgment by not contacting the sheriff? *No!* she said to herself. *The only law I live by is the backwoods law I make for myself.*

With each step she took, hatred engulfed her vulnerable heart. Forgiveness was unremitting; mercy was unrelenting. What would confronting Creel solve? Would she face him down? Perhaps even shoot him? She tried not to yield to a quick-fix mentality.

Fervently, Katie began to pray for a solution. Her decision to seek a spiritual resolution became her priority. Would the good in her prevail? Would she surrender to a forgiving spirit, or would she succumb to the revenge in her heart?

Up ahead was a flicker of light coming from the hobos' campfires. Upon reaching the trestle, Katie noticed an old man sitting alone in the crisp air, rubbing his hands together in an effort to warm them over the smoldering coals. Drowning his woes and sorrows, he emptied the last drop of whiskey.

Tucking her hair further underneath the hat, Katie pulled the collar of the coat up to conceal a slender neck. Under the long trench coat, the shotgun was obscured.

With eyes half-cocked, the old man, not quite succumbing to the booze, looked up at Katie. He held up his jug. "Would you like a snort?"

Katie shook her head. She wasted no time in saying to him, "I'm looking for Creel Burr."

The old man spat into the fire. He thought for a minute, rubbing his chin. "He told everybody on the river that a beautiful young woman with blond hair would be coming by. Did you really think that no one would notice that you're not a man under all that garb?"

She ignored the callous comment. "Where is he?"

The old man stared as he carefully studied Katie. She remained as cool as the breeze that blew off the chilling waters of the Flint.

The hobo's brow furrowed. "Closer than you think, girl. Very close. Go on home, girl. Creel Burr is an evil man."

Katie replied, "I know." She cast a discerning look towards the sky. "It looks like rain."

The old man acknowledged her statement. Then he motioned to a big oak at the top of the slope near the tracks. Katie glanced in that direction. There stood Creel Burr!

Steadily, Katie walked towards Creel, who was casually leaning against the tree. Soon, the two adversaries stood face to face. Neither conceded; both stared coldly into each other's eyes. Creel's eyes were beckoning; Katie's were unforgiving. The only sound Katie heard was the crackling of the campfire.

Creel was not surprised to see this captivating young maiden from McAllister's Lane. Boldly, he spoke. "Well, if it's not Miss Katie McAllister." He spat. The saliva drooled down the stubble on his chin. "I knew that you would find me." Creel motioned Katie to sit. "Sit down by the fire. Warm yourself."

Katie stood, unyielding.

Creel shifted positions. The mere presence of this beautiful young woman stimulated his manly desires. It was evident that this devil yearned to push Katie into an empty and ravenous place.

Katie's fingers gripped tighter on the trigger of the shotgun, still concealed under the trench coat.

Creel chuckled, "Aw, don't worry, Katie. I ain't gonna try to do nothing. Not here, anyways."

One of Katie's hands held the trigger of the shotgun tightly. The fingers on the other hand dug deep into her flesh. The pain caused her to focus.

"Yep, Katie, you would have never found me if I had not wanted you to."

Creel's mood suddenly changed as memories forced him to take account of his life. "Let me tell you something about me," Creel began. "I've been ridin' these tracks up and down from one town to another all of my life, waitin' and watchin' for the right time and opportunity to…well, you know what I'm talking about. I ride the rails by night and search out the girls by day."

For a brief moment, Katie thought she saw sadness in Creel's eyes. Standing motionless and quiet, she allowed this wicked fiend to continue talking.

"I never knew any other life, and that's why I never settled down at any one place. I grew up in an orphanage, and let me tell ya, I grew up fast! You see, there was this director at the orphanage. Since I was no bigger than a grasshopper, he showed me all about what a man needs. Know what I mean? I had to bend over a washpot many a time for some grumpy old man to use me like I was some old sow."

For a moment, Katie felt pity for his demonic soul until he said, "Come on, Katie, come with me over there and let me show you what a real woman is supposed to do." He motioned towards the woods.

Katie grimaced; her gut churned. Her hand on the trigger of the concealed shotgun tightened.

Creel chuckled. "Are you gonna pull that shotgun you're trying to hide under that coat out and shoot me? Can't think of a better way to go. At the hands of the infamous Katie McAllister. Heard you could shoot a rat's ear off at twenty paces."

A sharp, burning sensation tinged Katie's throat, causing her to shiver. "I gave it some thought. But it's not for me to judge or to sentence. Only God is the core of justice. He's the only one who executes judgment." She turned to walk away. "Consider this your lucky day."

Was there anything he could say to infuriate this girl? Because he respected this spunky, independent girl from McAllister's Lane, Creel wanted desperately to keep her near. He thought it would be extremely gratifying to have her as his own. Before Katie could walk out of his life, Creel wanted one last chance to spark an interest so she would stay.

"Remember Rosie?" The fiend chuckled, licking his lips. "You and that boy should have never left her alone that morning at the river. Or at least you thought she was alone."

Katie felt her knees weaken. Trembling, a flush of heat swept through her body.

"I had to kill her," Creel continued. "She wouldn't stop screaming. I was scared you and Son would hear her and come back. So I put my hands around her throat to make her be quiet. But she kept on screaming. I squeezed harder. Then she was quiet and still."

At that moment, Katie's breaths were shallow, causing her to feel faint. However, she showed no emotion and continued to stare into his dark eyes. Would she allow this murderer to once again ride the rails and hurt innocent young girls? With every ounce of reserve, she forced herself to stand still and listen.

Creel didn't stop there. "I thought that ol' tree was gonna come crashing down when Jezra pulled down on his boy's legs to stop him from squirming. I thought he was gonna pull that boy's head off!"

Not realizing that she had raised the shotgun dead level at Creel's chest, Katie boldly said, "You are fixing to go to a sinner's Hell. Say good-bye."

Creel's eyes widened. He knew that he had pushed Katie past her limit. His eyes quickly darted around, looking for an exit. Across the trestle, he thought, to the black shantytown. She would never follow him there.

As fast as he could, Creel began running to the crossing. Across the ties he scampered, trying desperately to get away from Katie and the shotgun she held in her hands. Before long, he was in the middle of the tracks. Suddenly, he froze! A big, burly man stepped up on the tracks on the side where the black shantytown stood. Standing there like a mighty fortress with a big oak staff in his hands was Jezra King! Creel looked back at Katie, who was slowly approaching him from the other side, shotgun held high and aimed directly at his chest, then back to Jezra, whose legs were staunchly held wide. Below was the river—water not deep enough to dive from this height.

In the distance, the whistle from the locomotive's engine blew. The roar of the train and the blast from the steam whistle grew louder.

Sandwiched between Katie and Jezra, Creel had nowhere to go. He crouched as if he was going to jump. Something made him change his mind. Instead, he turned to face Katie, darting towards her as fast as he could. The rumble and clatter of the steel wheels on the rails became louder, as did the sound of the train's whistle blast. Jezra jumped to safety just in time. Suddenly, Creel stopped! His cold eyes met Katie's. In the last moment of his life, he smiled at Katie as he deliberately fell backwards onto the railroad tracks.

As Katie jumped to safety, the cow catcher on the front bumper of the steel engine pushed Creel over the side of the trestle. The train rumbled past. Katie's nostrils flared; her eyes stung. It was only at that moment that she realized that Creel Burr was gone!

Stoically, Katie stood as if in oblivion. She stood until she could no longer hear the sound of the locomotive clanging down the tracks. Everything was quiet and still. Finally, she blinked her eyes and mumbled, "Live by the rails, die by the rails."

Katie glanced across the river. The tall trees on the other side rose out of the haze, meeting the less than dismal cloudy sky. Her eyes came to rest on Jezra and Sadie King standing arm in arm. Both triumphantly raised their arms above their heads, index fingers pointing up—a victory signal! Katie did the same.

In the quietness of the moment, Katie walked to Creel's fire. She was in ultimate control, no frailty. As the flower turns to the sun, Katie turned to the heavens, lifting her heart in the spirit of earnest prayer. Feelings of helplessness unraveled as tranquility subdued the storms in her fragile heart. Silent sorrows became small triumphs.

"Dear Father," Katie began, "I surrender to You and rest in Your trustworthiness. I know that You will see me through, for I am in Your hands. I trust that You will walk with me through trial."

Rubbing her hands together, Katie warmed them near the hot embers. The dismal and dreary sky disappeared along with the distant rumbles of thunder.

As the sun lifted its head, a golden radiance poured forth. The effect of the warm, glowing hues was so stunning that it overwhelmed her senses, leaving her breathless.

At that moment, Katie noticed a knapsack lying on the ground. It had belonged to Creel. Inside were a coffeepot, a razor, and a piece of a broken mirror. As she fumbled around, she pulled out a cloth bag sewn from a flour sack. Nervous hands untied a piece of twine that tightly bound the sack. Inside, bound with thread, were locks of hair. All were different shades, mostly blond. She picked up the lock that was reddish blond and held it the palm of her hand. It belonged to Rosie. Suddenly, it felt like hot coals. As she slung the locks of hair into the fire, she looked up from the flames.

"All is well, Rosie. All is well, Son. It is resolved."

Chapter 7

A PLACE TO HEAL

Going home gave Katie a sense of peace. God would provide deliverance from the evil and sorrows that had transpired. His providential, sovereign care was evident in His plans for her. Although Katie was fragile at this point, she would wait, trust, and have faith that He was in control. God's care was eternal and Katie knew that He would deal with her compassionately.

For a season, Katie remained on McAllister's farm. Alone and isolated, she ate only from the land and the garden. She felt it best to stay inaccessible until the necessary healing came to pass and until her father came home. Too much bitterness, too much blame, and an unforgiving spirit had caused Katie to distance herself from those whom she held in contempt. A bonded relationship with friends and neighbors had been broken, leaving only heartrending memories, tears, and loneliness.

Katie's heart yearned for Sadie, who possessed a wonderful gift for making each battle with even the smallest adversary a victory in a much greater war. She knew that Sadie would help her fight the battles that raged deep within her soul, the place where an avenging heart festered. Sadie had taught her that the core of a person's life was a propensity to love and the ability to practice forgiveness. During Sadie's absence, Katie kept these thoughts is her mind and prayed that Sadie would do the same for herself.

Quietly and serenely, Katie, now eighteen years of age, waited to find within her the faith and trust she once exhibited. At this point in her life, she felt that bitterness and hatred had poisoned her very core. As she continuously struggled with these negative feelings, she prayed to become enlightened and find comfort and peace and to renew her faithfulness.

Many lonely hours spent walking the rolling hills and green meadows calmly settled her spirit as she remembered that forgiveness for others came only when one felt forgiven. Riding over the land she loved from atop the mule's back, she saw the terrain as she never had seen it before. Trees grew tall, seeming to nudge the sky. Rich and fertile land once made soft by the breaking of the plow irons lay on the hills that surrounded the majestic woods, ready and waiting for tilling. The land had a beating heart of its own. It was as if the one sovereign Creator's mighty hand had swooped across this place and, with His gentle pat, had perfected the ground so neither man nor mule would strain with the plow.

Katie's favorite place to spend time reflecting was the river's edge. Soothed and relaxed, she would lie stretched across the cool sandbar, basking in the warmth of the golden sun. The sandbar was her island of tranquility amid the vortex of a sad and angry world. It was her place of refuge where mistrust and hatred were forgotten. It was her place to reconnect and restore faith in God's love and grace. Gradually, her heart began to mend. An unforgiving spirit slowly flowed away like the gentle waters of the mighty Flint River.

As Katie waited for the return of her loved ones, she did not allow the trials she endured as an excuse for idleness. Busily, she continued working the land as her father would have done. Katie always loved to turn the soil with the plow. The quietness and solitude of the land as it was being worked, the constant plodding of the mule, the creaking and clanking of the harness were peaceful to her. Occasionally, she would stop and scoop up a handful of dirt made soft by the breaking of the plow iron. The soft, friable earth would crumble as she held it to her nose. The distinct fragrance of the freshly turned, mellow ground was something that only a daughter of the soil could appreciate.

One such evening, after a long day of work, Katie led the mule to the barn, unharnessed him, and emptied a bucket of fodder into his trough. She rubbed his back.

"You did a good day's work, ol' boy. You never complain, and you never talk back!" She giggled at thought that this animal of toil might actually respond to her. "I know you don't understand anything that I say, but I have to talk to someone or I'll go crazy. You are all I have."

As Katie walked to the house, she caught sight of a keen chicken hawk perched high on a tree branch amid an open field of grass and thick briars. The hawk's piercing eyes spied a lone squirrel scampering along the edge of the trees. Swiftly and gracefully, the hawk lifted its wings and dove for its prey. Up into the open heights above, it carried its meal away. It was a pointed reminder that the circle of life continued.

Dreamy eyes came to rest on the horizon down McAllister's Lane. In the distance, there was a blur; someone or something was moving towards her. Grabbing her rifle, she anxiously waited and watched. The object was slowly moving closer and closer.

"Looks like a man walking this way," Katie whispered. "Don't know who it could be." She cocked the rifle. "But he'd better be able to run!"

Just as Katie raised the rifle and aimed strategically at the ground near the intruder's foot, the man yelled, "Don't shoot me, girl! It's your pa!"

Katie gasped. "Papa!" she yelled. As she laid down the rifle, Katie began running down the lane, slow at first, then faster and faster, straight into the arms of Thomas McAllister!

For a while, they embraced; neither wanted to let go. Secure in her father's arms, Katie said, "Papa, I've missed you so much."

"I'm home now, Katie, and I am never leaving my little girl again." Bending his tall frame, squared with broad shoulders, Thomas lovingly kissed Katie on top of her head. With tear-stained eyes, she looked up into her father's face, the white teeth encased in a square jaw and graying hair falling over to the side.

Thomas held Katie at arm's length and turned her around and around. "What happened to my little girl? You've grown up on me!"

"Oh, Papa."

"Don't 'oh, Papa' me! I'll be beating the boys off with a stick before long!" Thomas's brow furrowed. "And what's this I saw down at the end of the lane, Kat? I see where you have built a barricade across the road and nailed up a sign that says, 'Trespassers will be shot.'"

Katie did not respond, confident that Thomas would understand. Instead, she asked, "Did Jezra find you? Did you see Sadie? When are they coming home?"

"Hold on, girl! One question at a time! Yes, Jezra finally found me. He did exactly as he told you he would do. He looked down every street until he found me working at a livestock barn. The man I worked for paid me fifty cents a day, one meal a day, and a place to sleep—in the hay loft!"

"And what about Jezra?"

"As luck would have it, Mr. Thoms, the man I worked for, let Jezra take my place."

"What about Sadie?"

"Sadie got lucky, too. She's a maid and cook for some rich ol' lady who never trusted banks." He chuckled. "She doesn't get paid a salary, but at least she gets to take home leftovers every day." He paused. "Jezra told me everything that happened here. I mean with Son and all."

Katie nodded. Still, reminders of the past events were painful.

Thomas continued. "I'm sorry, Katie, that I was not here for you. I should never have left the farm. If I had been here, things would have been different."

"Don't blame yourself, Papa. What happened has happened. It's not your fault. But I do know who is to blame, and I *will*—"

Thomas stopped in the middle of the lane. He turned to Katie, forcing her eyes to meet his. Gently, he cupped her face with his calloused and weather-beaten hands. "No, Katie. Listen to me. It's time that all this blame and hatred and self-pity stop."

There was a deep sigh. Katie chose to remain silent; she was not certain that her father could understand the hatred in her hurting heart.

"I realize that it is difficult to forgive those men who killed Son. And I understand how hard it must have been for you to experience that awful tragedy." Thomas pulled Katie close before he continued. "All I know is that I love you too much, Katie, to continue to stand by and allow you to put yourself in a place of imminent judgment. You see, Kathryn, one has to forgive to be forgiven."

Thomas wrapped his arms around her. Slowly, they walked arm in arm down the road; each step was defined and taken with a sense of hope. He went on to say, "You know, Kat, all of us are affected by what happened to Son. Me, you, Sadie, Jezra. We all feel betrayed. The Bible doesn't tell us that we shouldn't feel angry. However, it does tell us that we should handle our anger properly. Don't give Satan an opportunity to destroy you. Instead of acting the way the devil wants you to, forgive others just as God has forgiven you. The Good Book says to be kind to one another, forgive one another even as God has forgiven you." He stared off into the distance. Then he commented, "I don't know enough about all of God's love. But I do know that God's infinite love and forgiveness can help you forgive others. He gave us an immeasurable gift when He died so we could be forgiven. And our response should be offering forgiveness to others; regardless of the wrong they have done us. Because of His great love for us, His Son died to save wretched souls like ours. It was His life for ours. It was His blood instead of yours. On the cross, those were His nails, not yours."

Once more, Thomas turned his daughter to face him. The wise and God-fearing man, sound in doctrine and focused on the Word, continued to encourage her. "Love your neighbors just as God acted in love when He sent His son to die for your sins. Forgive because you are forgiven. Give your grief and your hatred over to Him, Kat. He'll carry the load."

With much love and admiration, Katie smiled up at Thomas McAllister. Tears welled in her eyes as she became overwhelmed with the compassion and understanding this man displayed. How could she have ever doubted her father's empathy and concern?

"The time has come for you to come out of hiding and to get out in the world again," Thomas said. "It's time to forget, Katie, and more importantly, it's time to put the past behind you. You can't live out here like a hermit anymore. The barricades need to come down."

Thomas's words emboldened Katie's fractured heart, reinvigorating her with the realization that she desperately needed to find a way to obtain grace and favor in the sight of God. Like the sweet peace of the flowing waters at the river's edge, her spirit was renewed. Katie's tongue cleaved to the roof of her mouth. Her body became numb. The stumbling block was removed; her soul was delivered.

The next morning, father and daughter walked side by side, holding hands, back down McAllister's Lane, the place of remembrance of family loyalty and perseverance, and the place where God's words were honored and held in high esteem. The barricade was torn down. A new sign was erected. It read, 'All visitors welcomed.'

Chapter 8

GRATEFUL HEARTS

*D*arkness faded as rays of a glowing morning sun filled the radiant sky with solemn purples and ambers, and yellow and orange rays. The roosters sparred for dominion over the yard. The winner flapped its wings and crowed loudly, announcing his victory. The loser limped away, defeated and ashamed.

Thomas looked at the small garden Katie had strategically placed behind the barn where the soft, pliable earth exposed the plants to the morning sun.

"Seems like all we're going to have to eat around here is sweet potatoes."

Katie laughed. "We're going to sell them, Papa. And what we cannot sell, we'll barter. And what we don't barter, we'll feed to the livestock."

"So you are an entrepreneur of sweet potatoes, now, are you?"

"Yep. We have to learn to readjust because of this darn Depression."

"I know. Cotton has always been our mainstay crop, and it's useless to put something in the ground if we can't make a profit. Last I heard, cotton was only a nickel a pound,"

"However," Katie began, "sweet potatoes have multiple uses. If we can't sell 'em, we can eat 'em. Or at least the hogs can!"

Thomas watched his daughter as she cut the potato vines into strips. "Why are you cutting the vines like that?"

Patiently, Katie showed her father how to cut the vine beneath a leaf where a nodule grew. Pointing to the nodule, she said, "This will sprout, take root, and grow a new potato." She held up a piece of vine that she had cut. "I call these draws."

Thomas scratched his chin. "So this is what you have been doing with all your time?"

"Somewhat." Katie grinned. "The draws from this little patch of potatoes will produce a field."

"So we are sweet potato farmers now," said Thomas, clearing his throat. He teased, "How can a man take pride in planting sweet potatoes for a living? I guess the King Cotton days are over for the McAllisters."

Thomas bent his tall frame. Katie lovingly kissed him on the cheek. "We plant potatoes because we can't get beans for planting cotton, my dear father."

Thomas took a piece of the vine out of Katie's hand. "How did you figure out all of this stuff? I mean about growing another potato from…"He wrinkled his forehead. "What did you call this?"

"A draw, Papa," explained Katie. "I call it a draw because the vine draws out to make another root. And I got the idea from watching Sadie root her cuttings to make more flowers."

"Well, I'll be a son of a gun," laughed Thomas. "I'm going to be a sweet potato farmer!"

Katie brushed her hands on her britches and laughed at her father's frivolity.

At that moment, the small brown calf bellowed from the corral behind the barn. Its beseeching pleas could be heard in the nearby woods, calling for its mother to respond.

Thomas McAllister said to Katie, "Kat, that ol' mama cow didn't come into the barn last night to feed her baby. The way that little fella's sides are caved in, he has not sucked this morning, either. Maybe you ought to ride down into the woods and see if you can find our herd."

The McAllisters had a small herd of sixteen cows and one bull. Because there was a no-fence law in the county, a farmer's herd of cows could roam the open woods and forage for food. When a cow gave birth to a newborn, the calf was kept in the barn. The calf would bawl when it would get hungry, and the mama cow would come in from the woods to feed her baby. A bell tied around the mama cow's neck rang as she walked. The other cows, accustomed to the sound of the bell, would follow her home and would be corralled for the night. In the backwoods of

South Georgia, putting a bell on the lead cow was the only way to keep the herd together.

"Yeah, before Son was—" Katie stopped. "Mr. O'Hara caught some ol' boys from the other side of the county cutting their notch in the ears of his cows. They were driving 'em back to their farm, claiming that Mr. O'Hara's cows belonged to them."

"I'll get you a mule," said Thomas. "There are a lot of hungry people roaming around the country these days. You can't blame a man for stealin' some meat to feed his family, but I'd rather give them the meat than have them steal it from us."

"You're not going with me?"

"No. You can find the herd on your own."

"What are you gonna do?"

"My sweet, inquisitive daughter, I am going to start getting the sweet potatoes ready to plant." Thomas looked up at the sky. "Looks like we might get a shower later today. I'd like to have them in the ground before it gets wet."

Thomas brought a mule to Katie. She jumped on the big sorrel's back. Thomas handed her the rifle, and across her shoulder, Katie slung a rope.

"Never know if I'll have to hog-tie that mama cow and pull her home," she replied.

Katie kicked her mount in his side and galloped off towards the wooded area of the farm. Within the woodland of the McAllister farm, magnificent hardwoods and long-leaf yellow pines grew. However, deeper in the woods, growing near the creeks in the lowlands, knotty-kneed cypress towered towards the sky. A cow could easily lose its way or find a slow, murky death stuck in the mud. Man or beast could fall into a suffocating death of shifting sand lying in wait to swallow up and consume its helpless victims.

Deep in the woods, Katie saw tracks, the soil still pliable and undisturbed. She traveled in the same direction as the herd, following the wire grass. Along the way, she noticed beds rooted out by hogs under the underbrush. She wondered why she could not hear the bell. Katie looked worried.

"Something is not right."

She tilted her head and strained to listen. Other than the noisy chirping of song sparrows, she heard a faint, unrecognizable sound. She decided to walk a piece, keeping her ears and eyes open. Carefully, she crept through the woods. Occasionally, she would stop and listen to sounds she did not recognize. Suddenly, there was someone moving among the trees. She crouched and moved in closer.

Ahead in the bush among the palmetto, a middle-aged man and a woman had managed to hoist a dead cow by its hind legs to a pole placed between two forked trees. The man was making crude attempts to skin and gut the cow. The McAllisters' cowbell from the lead cow hung from a limb near their homemade scaffold.

Katie remembered the movement she had seen earlier in the trees a few minutes ago. She thought, *There's still another one out there. Maybe when I go in, I'll flush them out.*

The couple, smudged with dirt and cow's blood, looked as if they had not bathed or eaten in a long time. The trespassers might or might not be dangerous, but most definitely they were hungry!

Slowly, Katie walked into their camp. The couple did not hear her until she was directly behind them and spoke.

"Morning, folks. Need any help?"

Startled, the pair jumped. The man reached for a long staff, which appeared to be his only weapon other than the knife he was using to butcher the cow. The woman, eyes wide in fear, crouched down. She trembled, unsure of their possible assailant's intentions.

"Hold it, mister. Don't be so quick to grab that stick," said Katie. Remaining calm, she pointed to her rifle.

The man froze in his tracks. He,too,totally distraught, began to tremble.

For a moment, Katie pitied them.

The man stuttered as he lowered his head, avoiding Katie's eyes. "We were desperately hungry. I'm terribly sorry if we have done any wrong."

Katie noticed that he spoke elegantly and not in the traditional Southern vernacular.

"Do you even know how to butcher a cow?" she asked.

"Not really."

Katie looked at the dead cow hanging from the scaffold. As she closely inspected the animal, she could tell the man lacked expertise in butchering.

She asked, "Have you ever butchered a cow before?"

Humbly, the man answered, "No."

Katie shook her head, sighing in disgust. Still, the man and his wife avoided her eyes.

She walked over to the tree limb where the bell was hanging. Each neighboring farmer cast his cowbells to a different pitch so that the sounds would be different and distinct. The McAllisters' bell was a thick cast. Katie rang the bell. The tone was deep and dull. It was definitely the McAllisters' cowbell.

Slowly, the woman moved closer to her husband. Her soft face, encased in unkempt hair, looked as if it was unaccustomed to harsh weather. Her hands, dirty and bloody, were not calloused and hardened to work. Wide eyes suddenly darted to the right and then quickly back to Katie. It was obvious that the woman was hiding something or someone behind the trees.

Katie glanced towards the trees where the woman had glanced. "You'd better come out from behind that tree," she shouted. "There's a big hollow at the bottom, a good place for a cane rattler to hide."

The bushes rattled. Quickly, a small, frightened child scampered out from behind the tree and into her mother's arms. The woman grabbed her little girl and held her close to her bosom.

"Are there any more of those hiding in the bushes?" Katie asked the man.

The man nodded. "Come out, son. It's okay."

A young boy slowly emerged from behind another tree where he had been instructed to hide in case strangers appeared.

"How old are your children?" Katie asked.

"Grace is ten, and Will is twelve," answered the mother as she pushed her children behind her as if trying to protect them.

Katie sensed her fear. "I'm not going to hurt you or your children. I just want to know who you are and where you are from." Then she added, "And I'd like to know why you killed one of my cows." She walked over to the dead cow and picked up the cow's ear. "See this notch? This mark is the McAllisters' mark." She sighed. "Sir, it's a crime in these parts to steal and butcher someone else's livestock."

Ashamed, the man lowered his head. At a loss for words, he made no reply.

The woman, hiding her children behind her skirt, spoke first. "My name is Ann." She motioned towards the man. "That is my husband, William. We are the Hamptons."

"What are you doing all the way up here in South Georgia? And why are you camped out like a bunch of scoundrels hiding in these woods?"

The wife continued, "My husband was studying to be a doctor. I was working in a sewing factory to help him through college. When the Depression hit, the factory closed. He had to stop with his education to look for a job but couldn't find one. Finally, what money we had saved was gone. We lost everything." Sadly, she added, "These are impoverished times."

"Yeah, and sometimes, it's sad to say, those who do not lack material wealth are those who are the most impoverished."

William quickly retorted, "May I say, Miss..."

"Katie. Katie McAllister."

"Miss McAllister, we may be impoverished, but we are humble. We may be facing disappointments and lost dreams and live with unmet needs, but we are a godly family. The Lord has always honored us for helping our brothers and sisters when we had the means."

Katie laughed. "Don't get your feathers all ruffled, Mr. Hampton. I wasn't making any reference to you. But it's a good thing to know that you and I stand on level ground and have a mutual understanding that immaterial wealth is accessed when we encourage and help one another regardless of need. Knowing where you stand will help me make a decision on what your punishment should be."

"Punishment?"

"Punishment," Katie repeated. "By the way, how did you end up here? I mean on this land?"

Mrs. Hampton answered, "I have family who live in Birmingham, Alabama. We thought that if we could get there, we could stay with them, and we would be all right." Her soft face wrinkled into a frown. "We didn't have any money for train tickets, so we did as most families are doing these days. We jumped on a boxcar and planned to ride the rails to Birmingham."

"Why didn't you stay on the car? Why did you get off?"

"All we carried with us was what we could carry on our backs." Her eyes filled with tears. "Except for Pooch." She gently rubbed her son's tangled hair. "Pooch was Will's little dog. Will couldn't leave Pooch behind, so he brought his dog with us."

The little boy named Will buried his face in his mother's shoulder. His frightened eyes blurred with tears. Embarrassed, he quickly wiped them away with the back of a dirty hand.

The mother continued. "We were on a car with other families. They refer to them as family cars...I mean the boxcars on which hobo families ride. Anyway, I suppose those people hadn't anything to eat lately, either." She paused. "They took Pooch from my Will and..." Ann choked back agonizing tears as she remembered Pooch's demise.

William added, "When the train stopped in the town called Sylvester, we slipped off. We thought we would eventually catch another train. But there were no more trains. It was my idea to start walking. I thought we could find food in the woods. Rabbit, squirrels, anything. I guess we traveled farther than I thought. Soon we were lost."

"I left good tracks," stated Katie. "Follow them back to McAllister's Lane. You can stay in the old tenant house."

The poor, distraught Hampton family huddled together, not understanding Katie's intentions.

"You can stay on the farm for a while," she explained. "My papa's name is Thomas McAllister. Tell him what happened. He'll show you where to sleep." Katie grinned. "You can start work today. My papa has some sweet potatoes to plant. He'll be glad to have some help."

The confused man frowned. "You are kind to offer us hospitality, but as soon as we are able, we'll be on our way to Birmingham."

Katie grabbed the mane of the big sorrel and pulled herself up. "No sir, I don't think so. You won't be leaving for Birmingham anytime soon. What you did today is a hanging offense in the backwoods of South Georgia."

The man pulled his frightened family closer.

Katie grinned. "But since we make our own laws in these parts, I suppose about two months is sufficient enough time for working out the value of that cow."

The anxious man's tense muscles relaxed, as did those of his family. Even though this sudden change of events was unsettling, Katie's calmness assured them that they would not be harmed.

As Katie glanced over to the poorly butchered cow, she chuckled, almost to the point of sarcasm. "And you were studying to be a doctor?" She kicked the mule in the side, tipped the brim of her hat, and galloped off to find the rest of the herd.

Astonished, the Hampton family watched Katie McAllister disappear into the tall trees.

"Hmmm," began William. "Ann, I honestly believe that we do not meet people by accident. Sometimes, they cross our paths for a reason." He wrapped his arms around his distraught wife. "I wonder what this reason will be."

Chapter 9

BETWEEN TWO NATURES

$\mathscr{K}$atie rode deeper into the woods, tracking the lost herd. Recognizing the marking on a nearby cypress tree, she knew that she was on another man's property. Three parallel slants, top ends pointed toward the southwest, slashed deep into the tree, indicated that she was no longer standing on McAllister's land. The markings designated the property line between Whiskey Jones's and the McAllisters'.

Jaw tightening, Katie cringed and slightly shivered. Whiskey Jones was one of the men who had participated in the hanging of Son King. As she turned to go, sudden sounds of distress in the near distance caused her to stop. Slowly, she climbed down from the big sorrel's back. Cautiously, she walked in the direction of the sound of a frantic voice anxiously calling out. Within a short distance, she found the source of the distressed wailing.

Emotionally and physically exhausted, Buster Reese, one of the members of the irate mob that night, was chest deep in a pit of quicksand!

Holding onto a pine sapling caught before his slow descent into the soft, shifting sand, Buster Reese pleaded, "Help me! Somebody, please help me!"

Katie ambled her way to the edge of the murky pit. Carefully and slowly, she squatted as she laid the Henry rifle on the ground along with the rope slung over her shoulder.

Kneeling down to greet her undesirable foe, who was seemingly neck deep in misery, she toyed with him.

"Howdy, Buster. From my perspective, it looks as if you have gotten yourself into one heck of mess."

What seemed like the impossible had happened. Katie had found Buster in a situation in which ill feelings between the two could possibly be brought to a resolution. What a crowning achievement! Katie was certain her endeavor to convince Buster to choose wise relationships and make nondestructive choices would be inspiring and rewarding; that is, if she could convince him to substantiate her claim that his current life and actions held the key to a disastrous fate.

Buster, not sure if he was saved or doomed, shuddered at seeing Katie McAllister, the woman who had sworn to avenge the death of Son King. At this point, all he could do was beg. "Katie, please help me. I don't know how much longer I can hold on."

Buster's hands, red and swollen from his ordeal of grasping the green sapling, began to tremble. The bark from the tree, stripped because of Buster's continuous tugging, exposed white, fleshy wood that was becoming increasingly slippery.

Rather enjoying watching Buster Reese squirm, Katie made no immediate attempts to lend a hand. Instead, she chose to use this opportunity to convey to her enemy that he had the power to make choices in every realm of his life and that the truth underlying the right to make *good* choices was that one must live with the consequences.

Lethargically, Katie sat on the ground Indian style and began chewing on a pine straw. She teased, "Well, to tell you the truth, Buster, I'm not quite sure I want to pull your sorry ol' lard butt out of there."

Buster's eyes widened. He was doomed, or so he thought! Exhausted from his ordeal, he continued to beseech her sympathy.

"Please, Katie, please. I don't want to die. I've got my whole life ahead of me."

"Hmm, seems like I knew a boy not too long ago who had his whole life ahead of him." Katie spat out the pine straw she had crushed with her teeth. "He didn't want to die, either."

Buster writhed and whined. The shifting sand sucked him deeper. Suddenly, he began to sob, in much the same way a man would who knew his life was ending.

"I am so sorry about Son. I haven't been able to sleep since then. I have nightmares about that night all the time."

Buster's consistent wailing ushered in a sense of pity within Katie. Still, she remained committed to procuring the necessary change for Buster Reese. Coming face to face, she leaned over to her opponent and looked down into the muddy, shifting quicksand bed that could easily drag this man down to the depths of Hell's belly.

Once again, she grinned as she continued to toy with him. "I wonder how far down this pit goes? When a man is sinking down, I wonder if he tries to take a big gulp of air just before his nostrils and mouth fill up?"

Distraught, believing that death was inevitable, Buster squinted his eyes and fervently began to pray. "I promise, Lord, I'll never take another drop of whiskey again."

Katie frowned. "When did you start drinking, Buster? If I remember correctly, you never were one to partake of any rotgut." She sat back on her bottom and wrapped her arms around her tucked knees.

"Ever since that dreadful night, I have been tormented. I can't seem to sleep anymore. So I started drinking to help me sleep."

"You mean to ease your conscience."

"Yes, and that, too. That's why I'm in this mess now." Buster looked around at his dismal deathbed. "I ain't got any money to buy Whiskey Jones's booze. I was slipping around to the back of his still and gonna steal me a little hooch. That's when I fell in this quicksand bed." Once more, the poor, dejected man, uncertain of his future, began to feverishly pray.

Katie stood. "Hush, Buster! Hush with all that gibberish! The Lord hears you loud and clear!"

"Thank You, Jesus. Thank You, Jesus. Katie, does that mean you are going to help me?"

"Maybe. Maybe not. I'll see." Katie cocked an ear upwards, cupping it with her hand. "What did You say, Lord?"

Befuddled, Buster's contorted face gazed up towards the heavens, straining to see with whom she was conversing.

Katie continued with her playful strategy as she devised an inward plan to bring about an outward change in the life of Buster Reese. "Okay, Lord, I'll tell him."

"Tell me what?"

"The Lord said to tell you that a broad way leads to destruction, and a narrow way leads to life. And today is the beginning of a whole new chapter in your life if you learn to take the narrow way. That is, if you learn to make good choices, then He will make the change."

"Good choices?"

Katie's desire was for Buster to heed her words and for her words to penetrate his heart. She went on to say, "You made a bad choice when you stood by and allowed Son to be hanged that night. You could have intervened and done the right thing. But you made a bad choice and didn't."

"I'm so sorry, Katie. Truly, I am."

As she continued to recite the timeless truths and principles for Buster to follow, her tone softened. "Life is all about choices. And when you cut away the junk, every situation is still a choice. You were given a brain so that you would learn to make good decisions. If you would just stop letting the booze think for you, then every time some junk is thrown your way, you might do what is right."

Katie's voice softened further. "We live here in the deepest parts of South Georgia's woods where there is no law. When there is no law, faith is made void, for there is no transgression, only wrath. So we have to depend on faith and do what is right. And we have to earn our standing with the Lord by decisions that are honorable to Him."

Puzzled, Buster repeated his response. "Good choices?"

"Yes. And when you make those good choices, there is a sweet peace that comes. Oh, for sure, every day you are going to face problems, and there are decisions to be made. But Buster, the Lord allows that to happen to help you grow so that when you face temptations, you will know what is right and what is wrong."

"Okay."

She was not quite convinced that Buster might understand the complete and absolute truth concerning choices and consequences. "We all find ourselves where we have to decide to do what is right and proper, or to do things that are harmful and sinful. The way I see it, we can use our inner strength and the power of God to choose to do right and good, or we can give in to the ol' flesh, ignore the good, and choose evil. What I am trying to tell you is that our life is a result of the choices we make. It's sorta like between two natures—one good, one wicked."

Katie certainly understood the concept of the two natures she was trying to convey to Buster. During the worst of times, obstacles she'd faced had strengthened her faith, and her life had become an example of her own faith in action. Within the past few months, Katie had acquired spiritual progress as she built on the lessons of the past and moved into the future. The challenges she faced, as well as the decisions she made, were a major turning point in deterring the hatred that festered deep within her heart. Her newly acquired knowledge of and dedication to God's truth were eternal and never changing for the young woman of McAllister's Lane.

Buster, totally unaware of Katie's transformation, wanted to say what was necessary to appease her. He murmured, "Whatever you say, Katie. Whatever you say."

Katie continued, "Yep, Buster, and there is a thing called consequences. You know what I'm talking about? Paying for your sinful deeds. So if you make a choice, remember that your choices have consequences. Don't be deceived, Buster, because whatever you reap, you *will* sow. Consequences, so to speak. We don't often think about it, but whatever we reap is gonna follow us right on into eternity. And you just might end up going, well..."

"Save me! Oh God, save me!" Buster cried out. "Not from this pit that I deserve but from Your wrath and my damnation. Save me and forgive me!"

Buster lifted his eyes for God to send him mercy. Unknown to Buster, God already *had* sent mercy. Her name was Katie McAllister.

From Katie's perspective, it was a mission accomplished! Her profession of her faith passed easily from her lips as the application of her faith penetrated Buster's heart and entered his inner being. From henceforth, he would take his eternal soul seriously and make honorable, godly decisions. After all, right choices were his to make, and the consequences were his to reap.

The young woman, who calmly sat with knees tucked and chewed on pine straw, had accomplished what she had set out to do. She bridged the gap and restored an old friendship. More importantly, with all it entailed, she reconstructed human dignity for Buster and showed him the way to have a unique relationship with God.

"Katie, before I die, I have to tell you something. That night, I just got so caught up in all the hollering and all the booze that I just wasn't thinking clearly. And that stranger..."

"What stranger?"

"The leader. The man who wore that necktie thing around his neck. Had some kind of silver thing holding it together."

"It's called a bolo."

Katie, on all fours now, leaned down towards Buster, eyes narrowed, forehead furrowed. "Still, no excuses. You can't blame what you did on someone else. You have to assume responsibility for your own actions and not let somebody else define who you are."

"I ain't no good for nothing, Katie. I'll just go ahead and turn loose this sapling and go on down and be done with myself."

Katie sat back. "No need to do that, Buster. You are justifiably free. God forgave you when you asked for His forgiveness. It's in the past now. The slate has been wiped clean, and it is forgotten."

"You mean...? But, but...my sin was awfully big, Katie."

"Never minimize a little sin or overrate a big sin, Buster. They can all be forgiven. We have a mighty God, you know."

"What about you, Katie? Do you forgive me?"

"I can't declare you guilty. I can't judge you, pardon you, give you deliverance, or set you free. Your freedom was purchased, but not by me. It's God's mercy and grace, not mine."

Buster began to slip. "Katie!" he yelled. "Save me, Katie! Save me!"

"Land's sake, Buster. You are as dumb as a box of rocks!" Katie sighed. "I'm going to pull you out of this pit. But..." She paused.

Buster began to fidget, uncertain if Katie was true to her word.

"I will get you out of here, but only if you promise to do some things for me in return."

"Anything, Katie, anything! Just ask me, and I'll do it."

Katie rubbed her chin, contemplating her next move.

"First of all, Buster, you've caused a lot of pain and sorrow on McAllister's Lane."

"I know that I have."

"The way the Lord and I see it—" Katie motioned towards the sky, continuing to toy with Buster "—you've got to make up for your part in the wrong you did that awful night."

"Anything. Whatever you say, I'll do it."

"Sadie and Jezra King."

"Yes?"

"If you ever see them again, you are to treat them just as you would your own mama and papa—with kindness and respect."

"Yes, Katie, I will. I promise."

"And you've got to stop this drinking. You know it's not good for you."

"Yes, whatever you say. I'll stop."

"Besides, what happened that night is in the past. It is time we move on with our lives. It is time to put it to rest."

To Buster's dismay, Katie sat back down to mull over her next move. Reminiscing helped her to understand with clarity the events of that terrible night. She could not help but wonder about the man with the silver bolo slide. Who was he, and why had he been there?

Once again, Katie leaned over towards Buster. She began, "The more I think about it, Buster, the more convinced I am that the men involved in Son's murder were caught up in a big drunk. I think that you were pushed into the hanging without being given a chance to think about it. You allowed your liquor to think for you." She gazed pensively into the distraught man's eyes. "Despite what you did, you and the others were swayed, and I think that there was a man there that night who used booze to help manipulate and control all of you who followed him." She paused. "Am I right?"

"Yes, yes. He bought booze from Whiskey Jones and we got so tanked up, we didn't know what we were doing."

"Maybe you, the McKinnons, and Jackson Buford were tanked up. I'm not sure about Whiskey. I think he cooks that stuff so much he stays drunk on just the fumes. However, the strangers that were there with that westerner knew exactly what they were doing."

Katie was right, at least from her perspective. Katie thought more about the man with a bolo necktie with a silver slide at the O'Hara's house that night. He was Satan's imitator, the leader of that wild mob, who kept his followers mesmerized.

"Yes, he had an unalterable purpose to be at that cruel murder of Son King. But what was his purpose?"

Buster was quick to answer. "I don't know, Katie, I don't know. But I do know if you don't pull me out of here and soon, I'm a gonner. My arms are feeling like they are about to pull out of their sockets."

"Sooner or later. You still have a bit of juice left in you." Katie chuckled. "Tell me something, Buster. Do you know the name of the man wearing the bolo with the silver slide?"

Buster bit his lip. He wanted to recall every detail about this man for Katie. His willingness to talk could be the determining factor in how soon he would be pulled from this near death.

"I don't know his name. But I do know that he had been hanging around town a lot, trying to stir up trouble between white and black folks."

"So that Rosie O'Hara's death could cause further friction between the two races?"

Katie slowly stood. She tied the rope around the mule's neck. Slowly, she backed him close to the pit. Then, to Buster's dismay, once more she hesitated. "There's one more thing you have to promise me before I throw you this rope."

"Anything."

"Do you still keep dynamite in your work shed?"

"Yeah. Yeah. Yes, I do."

Katie continued to devise a plan. "Then this is the deal. Blow up Whiskey Jones's still. Blow it to Satan's Hell and back."

"But Katie, Whiskey Jones makes his living making hooch. Besides, he's a friend of mine. I couldn't do that to a friend of mine," Buster whined.

Angrily, Katie barked, "May I remind you, Buster, that I once had a friend? A friend whom you helped drag to his death! And you were liquored up on hooch, hooch that belonged to Whiskey Jones!" Her mouth twisted into a distorted frown. "I am giving you a chance to make amends. And if you don't take this opportunity, then you can rot at the bottom of that pit for all I care!"

Buster remained silent. He knew Katie was right and that he did not want to make her angrier.

With firmness, Katie demanded, "Blow the still to Satan's Hell, Buster, or I'll leave your sorry tail in that quicksand. No one will ever find you. And I will never tell. And you'll be soon forgotten." She turned to walk away, mumbling underneath her breath. Ignoring Buster's pleas, she clucked to the mule. "Let's go, mule. Doesn't make any difference to me if he sinks."

Buster realized this was his last chance to live or die a long, suffocating death. He yelled out to Katie, "Okay, okay! I'll do it!"

Katie stopped. Buster could not see the devilish grin that had slyly crept across her face. After all, she had to impart a little fear to keep him wary. Slowly, she backed the mule to the pit and threw the rope to the frightened man. With ease, the mule pulled Buster Reese free from his impending bleak death. Muddy and exhausted and with heart pounding, Buster lay panting on the ground.

Katie cocked an eye. "If two nights have passed and you have not blown up that still, I'll slip in on you at night in your sleep. I'll cut off your privates and feed 'em to my hogs!" She gave the mule a gentle tap on the rump and disappeared, leaving Buster Reese where he lay, thankful that he had been given another chance to make right choices.

Two nights later, Thomas McAllister and daughter Katie were sitting at the table, eating their meager meal. Suddenly, in the distance, there was the sound of a loud, jarring explosion. The foundation of the house shook. It was as if a mighty earthquake had sent shock waves through the earth's crust. Startled, Thomas McAllister dropped his glass of buttermilk. Milk splashed on the tabletop and floor. Glass shattered. As Thomas jumped up from the table, he knocked over his chair.

Befuddled, he hollered, "What the...?"

Cool and calm, Katie continued chewing her food. She held up her glass of buttermilk to make a toast. Devilishly, she grinned as she brought the glass to her lips. "Here's to making good choices."

Chapter 10

RETURN TO McALLISTER'S LANE

*T*he bullwhip cracked. The popping of the leather instrument of torment and pain rang loudly in the eardrums of the black man, tied helplessly to the big oak tree. As it lashed across his back, the unfortunate recipient of this heartless fate grimaced with agonizing pain. Face and body wet with perspiration, his knees buckled beneath the weight of his body. Clenching his teeth, he began to prepare for his inevitable fate.

Sadie King, kneeling next to her husband, pleaded, "Please, Mr. McKinnon, don't beat my man no more." Her eyes pooled with tears of overwhelming sorrow. As she reached her hands up toward Heaven, she prayed, "Oh, my dear Lord, please help us. We need You so much now." Finally, she fell in a heap on the ground and wept vehemently. Wet trails of tears left marks of desperation upon her cheeks.

"You black folks ought to stay away from these here parts. You ain't got no business moving back here to this place," barked the big, burly man with the bullwhip.

Another crack of the whip sent the stinking rawhide slicing into the bloody skin of its helpless victim. McKinnon's heinous, cowardly act was an embodiment of evil, a manifestation of wickedness spurred with unrelenting rage as his desire grew to dominate his victim.

Suddenly, from the ridge above, a rifle sent a bullet zinging past the man with the whip. Another well-aimed bullet struck the ground near the man's feet. Startled, McKinnon whirled around to see from where the shot was fired. Befuddled, he squinted against the sun's blinding rays as he quickly scanned the hillside. Signaling to his sons, Jamison and Addison, McKinnon encouraged them to quickly take cover. Hastily, they obeyed. Jamison darted for a tree. Addison sprinted to a secure place behind the black couple's wagon wheel.

"Who up there fired that shot?" McKinnon snarled, his heart palpitating. His nostrils flared as his gaze darted from one tree to the next.

"Don't know, Pa. It came from up top that ridge."

Joe McKinnon strained to see who was hiding behind the embankment. He shouted, "Who's up there, and what do you want with us?"

There was no answer—only dead silence.

McKinnon cursed. "Go on, now! You mind your own business! Leave us be to take care of ours!"

A woman's voice rang out loud and clear from the top of the ridge. "It *is* my business."

McKinnon cocked his head to one side. His tobacco-stained mouth twisted in confusion. He whispered to his sons, "That's a woman up there."

Jezra sighed, overcome with a feeling of jubilation. Just as he was giving up hope, he instantly recognized the woman's voice that rang clear from the hill. His taut, strained muscles relaxed as he realized his doom was not to be. Soon he would be free from this agonizing ordeal. A longtime friend had come to his rescue.

Sadie also recognized the voice of the young woman. She knew it well. "Thank You, Lord," she whispered.

McKinnon rubbed his rough, whiskered chin. He shook his head in puzzlement and whispered to Jamison and Addison, sitting crouched and trembling behind their havens. "One of you boys ease your way over to the pickup. Get that shotgun lying there on the seat. See if you can't work your way up behind her." McKinnon spat. Tobacco juice ran down the stubble on his chin. He wiped the drizzling saliva with the sleeve of his tattered and soiled red flannel shirt. "Better be careful, boy. If it's who I think it is, I'd rather tangle with a polecat."

Jamison and Addison cast a discerning look towards each other. Neither made a move to obey their pa. There was a terrible angst beginning to boil from the pit of their beings, a crippling tide of panic and dread.

Jamison whispered, "Pa, you thinkin' it be Katie McAllister? Katie McAllister from McAllister's Lane? 'Cause if it is, I'm staying right here. Right here behind this tree!"

The old man yelled to his oldest, "You mindless imbecile! She's just a girl! Don't tell me you're afraid of a dang girl!"

Embarrassed but still refusing to move, Jamison lowered his head. He turned aside the insults and sarcasm. . His father might think he had the intelligence of a Billy goat, but he was smart enough to remain well hidden behind the tree, his place of refuge. If it was Katie McAllister on that hill, it did not take a genius to figure out that he should stay well out of her range.

Addison concurred. "Pa, we've all seen Katie shoot her pa's rifle. She can split hairs with that Henry she carries."

Jamison added, "Purty well hits where she aims, Pa! You know we're right. We done got ourselves in a mess of trouble."

"Shut up, boys! Let me think."

Once again, old man McKinnon spat his chew. Fate would soon find its crooked path to this loathsome man. He mumbled, cursing under his breath as he leaned back against the big oak where he squatted. Fear arose inside out from a feeling of doom. His throat muscles squeezed tightly, and the sensation pounded into his perspiring temples. The worried look on his face told the story.

McKinnon knew all too well Katie McAllister was a person with whom he did not want a confrontation. It was true she could shoot a rifle and throw a knife more accurately than any man he knew. What worried him most was that he knew she had a score to settle with him and his sons, a score she'd sworn one day would be resolved.

"Pa, do you think that Katie is going to kill us?" Jamison asked. "Because we helped drag Son King to that tree and hung him?" Many nights, terrifying nightmares from a tormented sleep had awakened Jamison. Fragmented memories of the wailing from Son as he begged for his life had beleaguered Jamison's soul. Now, facing his avenger, feelings of shame and guilt held him bound in petrified hopelessness.

McKinnon took off his brimmed hat and wiped the perspiration from his balding head with his red, stained bandana. "Well, she said she was, didn't she? The night we hung that boy, she swore vengeance on the whole bunch." He bit into his bottom lip. "She said she'd come for us. She said what we did was above the law, and all of us would stand accountable." Fear festered in his heart; dread emerged from the doom that was to come.

Katie McAllister had indeed sworn vengeance on McKinnon, his sons, and the other members of the wild, frenzied mob that had murdered Son King. The irate mob, seeking backwoods justice, had dragged an innocent young boy to the Judgment Tree. That young boy was her friend. McKinnon knew well, as did other members of that crazed mob, that Katie harbored a complete and undeniable desire for retribution on the men she swore to kill.

Totally distraught, McKinnon wrinkled his nose and shaded his eyes from the blazing sun as it beat furiously on his head. From his vantage point, he could not see anyone, so he yelled up towards the top of the ridge, hoping to entice his would-be assailant to make her presence known. "Hey, Katie! Is that you up there on that ridge? Come on down and let's talk this thing over."

To his surprise, Katie answered. Her voice, clear and poised, called out from the ridge, "Nothing for me and you to talk about. Have nothing to say to you, McKinnon. But I would be obliged if you'd untie my friend from that tree."

The black man smiled. Bound wrists, tied tightly by a rope that swung over a huge tree limb, ached. However, he knew that the time of his pain's end and liberation was near.

McKinnon yelled up to the fiery woman whom he dreaded. "Katie! Thought you had left McAllister's Lane for good. Gone over Albany way to live. Yeah, folks around here thought we went on with these niggers here."

"Faulty assumption, Mr. McKinnon. I'm back. And have been for some time."

McKinnon swallowed hard as he shot an astute glance at his sons. "You're right, boys. We've done got ourselves in a mess of trouble. Yes sir. One big ol' mess. Guess we'd better scrape or die."

McKinnon motioned for Jamison to make a move. Jamison shook his head. However, Addison rose from his crouched position behind the black man's wagon wheel. Slowly, he eased out from behind the cover of the spokes. Another shot from the rifle from the ridge sent a bullet whizzing. The whining sound of the rifle bullet neared his ear. He shuddered. Quickly, he jumped back to safety from the infamous Katie McAllister.

"Sit tight, Addison. You're not going anywhere," said the woman from the ridge. "I'm asking you only one more time, Mr. McKinnon. Untie Jezra. Do it now, or I'll start shooting off ears!"

"Okay! Okay! But you come on down here, Katie, so the two of us can talk this thing over. Come on, now, and stop acting like this! I mean it, girl!"

"Mr. McKinnon."

"Yeah?"

"I'm through talking."

Suddenly the Henry rifle from above fired. A lone bullet snipped the tip of Joe McKinnon's right ear, which he instantly grabbed. At first stunned, he was now terrified when he saw the blood on his hand.

"Dang it, girl! What did you do that for?"

The silence was chilling, almost eerie.

Jamison and Addison's eyes widened. Astonished, their mouths twitched; their jaws dropped.

Jamison yelled, "I told you, Pa! You done gone and made her mad! You'd better untie Jezra or she's gonna shoot off your other ear!"

McKinnon quickly pressed his dirty bandana against his profusely bleeding right ear. "What did you shoot me for? You could have killed me!"

Calm and clear was the voice—unwavering. "No intentions to kill. Only want your attention. Now, untie the man. If not, I'll take your other ear."

Mr. McKinnon snarled, "You think you're so dang good with a rifle! You shoot like a man, so why don't you come on down here and show your face like a man? Or maybe you're scared like a girl and want to stay hidden up there behind your skirt tail?"

Slowly, the unscathed woman stood. The late afternoon sun, shining brightly from behind, made a silhouette of her figure. For a brief moment, Katie scanned the scene below. Then, with the ease and grace of a gazelle, she made her way slowly down the hill until she stood face to face with the old codger, McKinnon. Her blond hair glistened in the sun. A gentle breeze caught her long, flowing curls, causing them to dance atop her shoulders. Dungarees hung close to curvy hips. A white blouse opened at the top, revealing the long, slender neck of a girl who had come of age. Across full lips crept a sly smile. In her right hand was her papa's Henry rifle. In her left was his Fox double-barreled shotgun.

The McKinnon stood entranced and captivated. A skinny young girl had left McAllister's

Lane over a year ago. Standing before them now was an alluring and beautiful young woman. Joe glanced from the gun in her right hand to the gun in her left.

Katie grinned, sensing his thoughts. "One is never enough."

Jamison and Addison McKinnon were speechless, totally mesmerized.

Katie's gaze penetrated Jamison's, his eyes shining with lust like bright orbs, dancing with lurid thoughts meandering from his imagination. Calm and clear, her gaze unwaveringly beheld his. "In your dreams, Jamison. That's as close as you'll ever get." Jamison quickly averted his stare.

A quick glance at the light-skinned wife of the man hanging from the tree caused Katie's face to soften. She called out to her dearest friend. "Sadie, are you okay?"

Sadie King, with her husband Jezra, had left McAllister's Lane the day after their only child, Son, was hanged. Now they had returned, only to be met by the McKinnons, who wanted them nowhere in the vicinity to remind them of their malevolent deeds of that horrific night and the inconceivable murder.

Slowly, Katie eased her way to where Sadie was kneeling on the ground. Never taking her eyes off the McKinnons, she whispered to her beloved Sadie, "Have they hurt you?"

"No."

"Lucky for them."

Joe McKinnon leaned forward, straining to hear. "What did you say?"

In a louder voice, Katie shouted, "I said it's your lucky day, Mr. McKinnon!" More softly, she added, "Because if you had hurt one hair on this woman's head, you would be holding both ears and not one."

Quickly, Mr. McKinnon cupped his free hand over his uninjured ear. "Now hold on a minute, Katie. You don't know what you're doing here."

Katie replied, "I know exactly what I'm doing. I wouldn't lose one minute of sleep if I shot all of you down this very minute like

the dogs you are. It certainly wouldn't be a waste of humanity."
She eyed Joe McKinnon's unusually large and grotesque nose.
"Hmm, I wouldn't even mind rearranging that ugly thing you've
got sitting in the middle of your face."

Frowning at Katie's offensive remark, McKinnon rubbed
his nose. A desperate glance towards his sons beckoned them to
come to his defense. Not wishing a confrontation, the boys dis-
missed the summoning look. Obviously, they were too afraid to
disagree with the young woman from McAllister's Lane.

Katie motioned towards Jezra King, hanging by his hands
from the tree. McKinnon concluded that he did not have enough
hands to hold onto all of his facial appendages. With a quick jerk
of his head, he motioned Jamison to untie Jezra. Hastily, Jamison
moved to the tree.

As soon as the rope that bound his wrists was cut, Jezra fell
to the ground on his knees. Sadie scrambled to his aid. With the
hem of her dress, she gently wiped the perspiration from her husband's face.

"Help him get on his wagon," ordered Katie.

Jamison and Addison scurried to meet Katie's demands.

Katie's gaze remained glued to Joe McKinnon's. "Sadie, can
you drive those mules home to McAllister's Lane?"

Sadie nodded. "Yes."

"Go," Katie ordered.

Sadie covered Jezra's slashed and bloody back with her
shawl. She clucked to the mules, tapping one on the rump with

the leather strap. The mules jerked, sending them galloping into a dead run. Soon they were gone.

As soon as the wagon had rounded the bend, Katie motioned the three men to sit down. They were more than willing. Slowly, she squatted and picked up McKinnon's whip. Her gaze remained fixed on the loathsome three. "You still carry that pocket knife, Jamison?" she asked.

Jamison McKinnon smiled as he fondly remembered the times he and Katie had spent during recess at school pitching knives. He nodded. "Yes."

"Do you think you know how long three inches would be? Or did you nap when we were learning our measurements?"

Jamison stammered. "I think I do." The test was simple and infallible. However, he substantiated everyone's claim about his lack of mental faculties as he held up fingers indicating a distance not even close to three inches.

Katie chuckled as she shook her head. "You never were the sharpest tool in the toolbox, were you?"

Jamison grumbled. Insulted and angry, he made an attempt to stand. Katie raised the shotgun. Jamison shrank back and sank down to his crouched position.

"Sit tight, Jamison. Unfortunately, the last thing I want to do today is dig graves." She threw the leather whip to Jamison. "Start cutting! Three-inch sections."

"Aw, Katie, please," begged McKinnon. "That whip was given to me by my ol' man. I wanted to give it to one of my boys one day. Ain't no need to cut it up."

"Joe, I don't think you understand the situation that you and your boys are in at the moment. You have whipped your last man with that whip." She looked hard at Jamison. Her eyes narrowed and blazed. "Cut!"

Jamison jumped, more than willing to obey. Quickly, he began cutting the whip into three-inch pieces.

Joe McKinnon cringed and began to beg. "Katie, if you're going to kill us, then please go ahead and get it over with. Or else let me get to Doc Owens with my ear. It hurts bad. It's throbbing." He held tighter to the piece of meat that hung from his ear.

A faint chuckle emerged from Katie's mouth. It pleased her that Joe McKinnon was afraid and even feeling a little pain. "Sometimes a little hurting is good to make you understand the error of your ways. You know, I really wouldn't have to dig any graves. Right here and right now, I could kill all three of you, and by tomorrow noon, the buzzards would have picked your stinky carcasses to the bones." Mischievously, the feared woman continued to tease, "And you would never even be missed."

The McKinnons gulped. Fear resonated in them.

"Don't worry, Joe. You and your boys aren't worth killing."

"Whew," was their reply.

Katie contemplated her next move. It seemed to her that the McKinnons were in need of a little pruning and weeding—to bear not just fruit, but a harvest of service to others. "Hmm, tell you what I'm going to do," she began.

"What's that?" McKinnon asked. He cringed when Katie shoved the wide barrel of her shotgun close to his face.

"Failure to *hear* brings about a failure to *heed*, Joe, and if you don't hear what I say and heed what I tell you to do, then there is going to be a day of reckoning. A bad day!"

"Anything you say. Us McKinnons will do it."

"Widow McDonald," Katie began. "She's had a hard time since her husband passed a few years ago, struggling to put food on the table."

"Yep, she and her young'uns are surely having a hard time," replied McKinnon, trying to be as agreeable as possible.

Katie's eyes twinkled. She hoped that they couldn't see the obvious. Empowering the McKinnons with virtuous works and compassion for their fellow man was her plan, qualifying them for future blessing for kind and generous acts.

"This is what I want you and your boys to do, Joe. I mean, if you want to save your hides."

"What? Please tell us," begged Joe McKinnon.

"As long as that woman lives or any other woman left widowed around these parts, you and your boys are to keep fresh meat on their tables. And garden vegetables for their stew."

"Okay, no problem. No problem at all."

"Mrs. McDonald's roof leaks, and her porch needs fixing."

"As good as done."

"Do these things for as long as you live."

"Yes'm."

"As for Sadie and Jezra King…"

"Yes?" gulped McKinnon.

"Never look scornfully upon them or any people of color. When you meet Sadie King on the street, you treat her like she is someone special. Tip your hat and smile. If need be, offer your hand like a gentleman...because Sadie King is more lady than any woman you'll ever know."

"Okay. I promise me and my boys will do it."

"Regarding Jezra," Katie continued.

"Yes?"

"Don't ever let the plow break his back or cause him to strain from sweat and toil. Never say one unkind word to him, and *never* bring him harm."

"I promise, Katie, I promise." McKinnon paused. "But why? Why should we show respect to people of color?"

"We are all flowers in God's garden, equally the same. The same creator made us. Only the color of our skin separates us. Underneath the skin, there is no difference. Understand? Because you are white doesn't make you better than anyone else." Katie rose to her feet. "Well, not exactly, I guess."

"Huh?"

"Not all people have the same kind of heart."

"I don't understand."

"Some people's hearts are pure as gold, good to the core. Some, Mr. McKinnon, are just plain rotten."

"Me?"

"Not for me to judge, but if you say it to be true, then I guess it is. And while we're laying down some ground rules, let me add this: the next time you and yours stir up strife with me and mine…"

"Yes?"

"…there will be nowhere you can hide, nowhere you can go. I will hunt you down like the dogs you are, and when I find you, I will cut off that big, ugly nose that sits in the middle of that big, ugly face." Katie snickered. "And I'll use it for bait."

Joe McKinnon flinched and then grabbed his big, ugly, grotesque nose with his hand that was not holding his ear.

Katie showed no mercy until it came to Jamison. "Poor Jamison, your sweet mama is probably turning over in her grave worrying about you. Knowing that is punishment enough."

She kicked at the pieces of the bullwhip left heaped in a pile. "One last thing, Joe. You need to know that you and your boys hanged the wrong person that night. You took justice in your own hands before finding out the facts. McKinnon, you and your thugs executed an innocent young boy. Knowing that is going to be a hard thing to live with." Katie paused. "But you can't undo a done thing. All you can do now is try to make things better for the people you wronged. I'll be watching to make sure you do."

Stunned, the McKinnons looked at each other. Dismayed and ashamed by their unseemly participation in the execution of Son King, they asked, "What are you saying?"

"The ol' hobo, Creel Burr. The man who used to ride the rails and jumped off at McAllister's Lane is the man responsible for Rosie O'Hara's death."

"How…how do you know?" stammered McKinnon.

"He told me just before he died."

With the same grace and ease with which she descended, Katie climbed back up to the ridge's height. When she reached the top, her silhouette again showed distinctly against the darkening sky.

Mr. McKinnon yelled out to her, "Hey, Katie! Tell me. How did Creel Burr die?"

Stoically, Katie stared straight ahead. Slowly, she raised the Henry she clenched in her right hand. Mischievously, she grinned—a grin the McKinnons did not see.

The McKinnons shivered; fear rose in them.

Chapter 11

FLAMES OF FORGIVENESS

*J*ezra cringed. With a viselike grip, his hands tightly clenched the edge of the oak kitchen table as Sadie's trembling hands applied salve to the lacerations on his back, ripped and torn by the abhorrent whip of Joe McKinnon.

"I'm sorry, Jezra. I'm trying my best to be easy," said Sadie as her trembling hands gently rubbed on the soothing ointment. She glanced up at Thomas McAllister, who was pacing back and forth across the floor with heavy-laden and measured steps. "Mr. Thomas, sit down and quit worrying. You're gonna wear that floor out. Katie has everything under control." Sadie chuckled. "When Jezra and I drove off, a smidgen of Mr. McKinnon's ear was lying on the dirt. Ol' Joe was so scared that he smelt like he had dirtied his britches."

The corners of Thomas McAllister's mouth turned upwards in a smile, that of a proud father. He could not help but be amused at Sadie's comical remarks. Katie was certainly capable of taking care of herself. If anyone could make Joe McKinnon dirty his britches, she would be the one!

Thomas remarked, "She does have the savvy to equal any man." He began to relax and sat back down. "I bet ol' Joe did dirty his britches. He and his boys were here on the farm the day Katie shot off the tip of a match stuck in a fencepost. He's quite aware of how good that girl is with her Henry!"

For a brief moment, laughter filled the dimly lit room.

Suddenly, they heard the sound of a wagon creaking to a stop. Once again, Thomas bounded from his chair. As quickly as he could, he dashed to the back door. Katie pounded up the steps and ran straight into Sadie's outstretched arms.

With an emotional and deep-seated outburst, Katie cried, "Sadie, oh Sadie! You don't know how many times I have looked down that lane, watching and praying that you and Jezra would one day come home."

"Some homecoming, huh?" remarked Jezra.

"You know that I couldn't stay away from you forever, Katie," Sadie replied. She wiped tears that blurred her eyes with the hem of her apron. "You are my baby. No way in Heaven could I stay away from you." Tenderly, she brushed Katie's blond curls from her forehead. "It was just that after that night…" Sadie inhaled a deep breath. "Jezra and I thought that it would be best if we left this place. You know, because of what happened to our boy."

"I understand," Katie answered. "In my own way, I ran, too. But I learned something. You can't run away from things that you're trying to forget. It always has a way of catching up with you. "

For a while, the two women sat in silence, cleaving tightly to one another. Shortly thereafter, Katie asked, "Sadie, why were you and Jezra camped in that bottom?"

"We were coming in from Albany and had some trouble with one of the wagon wheels. We stopped there so Jezra could fix it. Just as he had finished, Mr. McKinnon and his boys drove up." Once again, Sadie hugged Katie as if she couldn't get her fill of showing her love and affection for the young white woman she had cared for since her infancy. "And thank the good Lord that you came along, Kat, or Jezra would have been a dead man. "

"Where did you get the mules and wagon?"

"Mr. Thoms, the man who your pa and then Jezra worked for at the livestock barn. He was such a good man to us. He knew how badly I wanted to come home to you, so he let us borrow the team with a promise to return them one day. "

Katie walked over to where Jezra was seated. She picked up his rough and calloused hands, accustomed to many years of hard farm labor. Tenderly, she held his hands in hers; her eyes traced each weathered line. Then she grimaced as she scanned his back, cut by the despicable whip of Joe McKinnon. A quick glance at Sadie brought awareness to markings of wet tear trails on her friend's soft, brown cheeks. Katie realized at that moment,

Sadie was remembering that harrowing night, a rope, and a horrific death, when she lost her only child.

Finally, the dreaded silence ended as Sadie softly spoke. "Jezra and I finally realized that just because a wrong was done to us didn't mean that we should always have hate in our hearts. No matter how hard we tried, we couldn't always live in our sorrows that seemed to be all around us. We had to try to close that door and live for today and not dwell on things of yesterday. We prayed that the Lord would heal our hearts, and He did. There was so much pain, Katie. But we learned that we can't and won't ever forget, but we *can* forgive. It doesn't mean what happened is okay. It just means that we had to make peace with the pain so we could let it go. For such a long time, my worries kept me up at night, all tied up in knots. Sometimes it was unbearable, but the good Lord showed me that He never meant for me to bear my problems all on my own. He was there with me, holding my hand and showing me His might and power. "

Sadie's merciful conviction stirred emotions in Katie's tender heart. "Oh, Sadie, you always did have a kind, forgiving spirit." Lovingly, she wrapped her arms around her beloved Sadie and squeezed her tightly.

Sadie continued, "There's enough hate in this ol' world already without people going around looking for it." As she helped Jezra put on his shirt, she added, "No ma'am. A soul can't worry none 'bout yesterday. All that does is just take away what little strength you might have to make it through the day that's already before ya. And besides, carrying hate in your heart takes away good things that might be coming your way. Anyhow, so that's why we decided to put it behind us and come home." Sadie looked at Jezra's back. "Maybe we should have stayed where we were." She searched the depth of Katie's eyes, hoping that she also had found peace.

Katie *had* found peace. She harbored no vengeance and had forgiven others so that God would forgive her. Despite the impression she had left with the McKinnons, Creel Burr's death had been accidental. Although she bluffed them earlier in the day, she had a genuine purpose—inject fear to teach the McKinnons a valuable lesson. They had to know that their heinous acts were wrong, and only the fear of Katie McAllister would ensure Sadie and Jezra's future safety.

She shared with the Kings the conversation between her and Creel shortly before he died. She told them how the memories of Creel's childhood had plagued him since he was a young child, held victim for the sexually perverted appetite of the director of the orphanage where he was raised. She shared how Creel's dark childhood had transformed him into a monster with dark desires, a man who became a prolific serial killer as he rode from rail to rail, victim to victim. A predicable yet disturbing routine had emerged—ride the rails by night, search for prey by day.

In her usual amiable fashion, Sadie said, "He should be pitied. "

Katie addressed the Kings. "Enough about Creel. Let's rejoice that you're here now. "

"I am glad, too," replied Thomas. "The best and safest place to be right now is in the backwoods like us, eatin' off the land. If a man owns a piece of dirt, he'll never starve."

"Yeah, and if a man don't own any dirt, he might have to eat some dirt to keep from starving," chuckled Jezra.

Laughter erupted within the room, and in the lightness of the moment, despair and gloominess disappeared. It was good to have Sadie and Jezra back home again. With Sadie home, a void in Katie's heart was filled. Once again, she was beginning to feel completely whole.

Suddenly, a loud knock at the door rang through the room. A desperate voice from the other side frantically yelled out, "Katie! Thomas!"

In a single stride, Katie scurried for the rifle. She quickly threw it to her father as she darted towards the shotgun leaning against the wall. Jezra grabbed a kitchen knife. Sadie picked up a rolling pin lying on the table. Within a few seconds, the McAllisters and Kings of McAllister's Lane stood armed, ready, and waiting for their intruder.

The intruder slung the door open! Eyes wide, he stood before his adversaries, not sure if he would be blasted into eternity. Trembling, the man standing before the McAllisters and the Kings was John O'Hara, father of Rosie!

Mr. O'Hara's throat muscles tightened when he saw the waiting arsenal, armed and ready to fight, standing before him. His voice quivered. "Please don't hurt me. I need your help. My place is on fire!"

Earlier in the day, sparks from a lone freight train had landed on brush near the tracks. After hours of smoldering, the sparks had ignited. A looming fire had slowly and deliberately crept towards the O'Haras' house. The O'Haras were in peril of losing their home. The McAllisters and Kings laid down their weapons and quickly scampered to the aid of one of the men who had hanged Son King.

At the O'Haras' homeplace, the three families frantically beat the raging fire with shovels and anything else they could find to squelch the looming flames. The stench of smoke burned their nostrils. They coughed to clear their lungs. Side by side, Sadie King and Betsy O'Hara, mothers of two deceased children, one white, one black, fought together to save the O'Hara home from the blaze that edged closer. In their efforts to work together fighting the fire, hatred gradually waned.

As the inferno neared, Thomas McAllister yelled, "Jezra, go back to our house and hitch up the mules! We'll plow a firebreak. Maybe it'll slow it down. "

Suddenly, a gust of wind burst forth. Fiercely, the flames whirled, and fire ensued. Sadie, beating the flames, backed into Becky O'Hara. Whirling around, she stared deep into the eyes of the woman who had struck the mule with a whip, causing the wagon that held Son to pull out from under his feet. For a moment, the two women stood silent and motionless. Katie watched as she held her breath. Confronting Betsy O'Hara the first time since her boy's death, would Sadie turn all of her sorrow and anguish towards this woman responsible for her son's suffering in such a heinous way? Or had she truly forgiven her?

Suddenly, without warning, consuming fire spread towards the shed. The flames danced, sending sparks twirling higher into the dark of the night. Everyone, including Sadie and Betsy, raced to save the building. However, in a matter of minutes, the shed, totally engulfed in flames, became a burning tinderbox. The luminous fire and the stench of the smoke sent neighbors from across the woods running to aid the O'Haras.

"Let the shed burn!" shouted Mr. O'Hara. "Help us save the house!"

By this time, Jezra had returned with the mules. He feverishly plowed a break to contain the skulking blaze. Others, using whatever implement they could find, laboriously continued to beat the flames.

Suddenly, Betsy O'Hara screamed, "Help me!"

The skirt of her dress caught on fire, sending hot, blistering flames flaring up the back. The closest person to Betsy was Sadie. Bravely, Sadie dashed to Betsy and threw her on the ground, rolling her in the dirt, suffocating the fire. For a while, the two women laid on the ground wrapped in each other's arms.

The small crowd stood still and watched. Each onlooker, marveling at Sadie's heroic efforts, wondered how Betsy O'Hara would respond. Slowly, Sadie stood and extended her hand for Betsy. Sadie pulled her once-despised foe to her feet.

Katie thought, *To apologize, you have to be courageous. To forgive, you have to be strong. In my heart, I know who is courageous and strong. Will the other one show mercy and grace?*

Unknown to them, a storm gathered. Lightning cracked as thunder clapped and rumbled. The dark sky opened its gut and threw upon the ground a hard, pelting rain. Large drops pounded the tired, weary people, bringing with them hopes that at least the O'Haras' home would be saved.

Soon the drenching rain covered the fire until it smoldered to a slow, fizzling death. Although the barn and surrounding buildings lay in a pile of charred remnants, the O'Haras' house remained standing, unharmed.

Katie tilted her face towards the sky, allowing the cool rain to wash away the smudge and soot. Then she turned to look for Sadie. Spying Becky O'Hara and Sadie King from afar, she watched. One white woman and one black were walking arm in arm towards the O'Haras' house. Through the worst of times, not so long ago, these women, adversaries in their own right, blamed one another for the deaths of their own children. Now, leaning on each other for support, the burning sting of hatred fizzled along with the smoldering fire. The powers of the chains of bitterness were broken. The storm had been weathered. Out of the ashes, the shackles of hatred had set them free.

Chapter 12

TIME FOR DISCERNMENT

Katie pulled back on the reins. "Whoa, mules."

The wagon came to a halt in front of Sadie and Jezra's house on the first bend of McAllister's Lane. For a moment, Katie sat on the wagon seat in front of the diminutive, wooden, shanty. Saddened by memories of happy days shared with Son stirred her malleable heart, causing welling tears.

Sadie flung open the front door. "Well, a fine good morning to you, Miss Prissy! Crawl down off that wagon seat. I've got some mighty fine biscuits fixin' to pop out of the stove."

Katie, rubbing her tummy, lifted her nose to sniff the delightful aroma of fresh-baked biscuits. Her gesture, showing that she was tantalized by the smell of Sadie's freshly rolled-out biscuits cooking in a hot oven, made Sadie smile. "Mmm, I can taste them now!" exclaimed Katie. Enthusiastically, she jumped off the wagon and bounced up the steps. "I'll be more than happy to partake of your fine cuisine."

"Hmm. You been hanging around that ol' Hampton man too long. You beginning to talk educated like him!"

In an instant, Katie had pounced into Sadie's cozy kitchen, eagerly waiting to be served a hot buttered biscuit fresh out of the skillet.

Sadie carefully bunched up the hem of her apron and took the biscuits from the oven. The aroma was alluring. Katie dawdled over to the wood-burning stove, impatiently watching as the fresh ham sizzled in a cast iron frying pan.

"Want a piece of ham stuck between two halves?" Sadie asked.

Eyes wide and bright, Katie nodded as Sarah cut a piece of ham and placed it the middle of the biscuit. "You're missin' my cooking, huh?"

"More than you know," Katie said, munching on crumbs that fell into her lap. She picked each one up and put it in her mouth. "Delectable!"

Sadie watched with delight, smiling with glee. "When you gonna let that poor ol' Hampton family go on 'bout their business to Birmingham? Then I can get back up in your kitchen and cook up some good groceries. Not that stuff called *food* Mrs. Hampton puts on the table!"

Katie lingered as she considered Sadie's question. "Probably soon. The sweet potatoes are planted. Growing good." Licking her fingers and savoring the last bite, she added, "I think that we've been mighty lenient. If William Hampton had been caught stealing anyone else's cow, he would have been horsewhipped for sure."

Sadie giggled. "Kat, you try to be so bad, but deep down in your heart and soul, you are as good as gold."

Katie jumped up from the table and pinched off another piece of ham. Then she playfully kissed Sadie on the cheek. "That's because I had a good as gold person raising me."

Sadie laughed as she watched with loving eyes the young girl she helped to raise from a baby. "You know, it was a good blessing the day you got dropped in my lap." She glanced out at the wagon parked in front of the house. "Well now, tell me, where are you going with that pig you've got tied in a crate?"

Suddenly, Katie remembered her purpose for stopping at Sadie's house. "Goodness, I almost forgot! Get your hat, Sadie. You're going to the general store with me."

"Now, what kind of business do you think we have at the general store? We ain't got no money to buy nothing!"

"We're about to run out of flour and a few other things. I'm going to trade that pig for some flour and..."

Katie spied Sadie's flour barrel sitting in a corner on the back porch. Just as she reached to lift the lid of the wooden container, Sadie screamed out, "No! Get away from there! No, I say!"

Frightened, Katie quickly snatched her hand back. "Good grief, Sadie! You scared the pee out of me! All I wanted to do was to look in your flour barrel to see if you needed some flour." She inspected the barrel closely. "Is there a snake somewhere?"

"Just get away from that barrel, Kathryn McAllister, and now!"

Befuddled, Katie obeyed. She watched as Sadie walked over to a second flour barrel sitting in the corner of the kitchen. Sarah lifted the lid and looked inside. "Yes, I do reckon I'm a' needin' some flour. I'll get my hat and shawl. I think it will do me some good to ride into town with you. Been wantin' to get out of this house for some time." She turned back to Katie. Her tone was sharp; her manner was brisk. Sadie snapped, "Well, let's go!"

Katie followed Sadie outside. All the while, she wondered why Sadie had become so frantic when she nearly opened the lid to the flour barrel sitting on the porch.

She hoisted Sadie onto the wagon seat. Then she hoisted herself on board and clucked, "Let's go, mules."

Further down the road, Katie cocked a discerning eye towards Sadie. She still did not understand why Sadie had yelled at her, especially over something as menial as a flour barrel! She attempted to give her an opportunity to apologize. "You know, Sadie, you didn't have to yell at me. I did no wrong."

"Maybe. Maybe not."

Katie would not be content until the issue was resolved. A few minutes later, she asked, "Are you sorry for yelling at me, Sadie? And over a silly ol' flour barrel?"

As the wagon jolted down the dusty road, Sadie's gaze remained fixed. Her eyes narrowed as she tightly clenched her fists on the shawl thrown around her shoulders. "Sorry? No! Not sorry! Not ever will I be sorry!"

When Katie and Sadie arrived at the general store, the street was lonely and empty. Weeds grew on desolate sidewalks where flowers once bloomed. Buildings where businesses once flourished were now boarded and barricaded, deserted. The Depression had certainly taken its toll upon this small southern community.

Katie pulled on the reins and brought the wagon to a stop in front of the grocery and dry goods, the only store remaining open for business. Transactions were conducted with no credit, only cash, or whatever anyone had of value that could be swapped or bartered.

To Katie's surprise, Buster Reese, the man she had pulled out of the quicksand, was standing in front of the building. Gentlemanly, he tipped his hat and nodded to both women. Then he walked over to the side of the wagon. Graciously, he extended his hand for Sadie. At first she was hesitant, inclined not to accept this newfound gentleman's offer to aid a lady. She looked at him rather curiously and then at Katie, who smiled and nodded, showing approval. Sadie kindly accepted Buster's hand. Buster helped her down from the wagon, tipped his hat again, and strolled off down the street.

Confused and surprised, Sadie stood shaking her head as she watched Buster Reese walk away. Puzzled, she finally spoke.

"Well, Lordy be, some things and some people never do stop amazin' me."

Although Katie remained silent, deep inside she beamed. She well knew the reason why there was a change in Buster Reese's behavior. Maybe Buster *had* heard God's voice that day in the quicksand and had asked Him to be his guide in making good decisions. In some respects, it seemed that Buster had learned that considering consequences and making sound judgments were necessary requirements in every decision one faced.

To Katie's satisfaction, Sadie's amazement did not end there. Inside the grocery, standing against the counter, were Mr. McKinnon and his two sons, Jamison and Addison. Upon seeing Sadie and Katie, Mr. McKinnon also tipped his hat in a chivalrous fashion. Almost within the same moment, he frantically grabbed his bandaged, severed ear. His sons stood with mouths open and jaws dropped, numb with disbelief or, perhaps, fear. A swift punch of his father's elbow in Jamison's side suddenly reminded the boys of their most recent lesson in showing respect and exemplary manners.

Unaccustomed to such gallantry, Sadie bowed her head and covered her mouth to stifle a giggle. Undoubtedly, she was pleased with the mannerly show of conduct even though she had no clue as to why these scoundrels were treating a black lady with such dignity. Still, Katie remained silent, careful not to intervene. Mr. Burley Todd, the clerk, looked up and across the top of his spectacles.

"Well, if it ain't Katie McAllister! Thought you folks had moved away. Haven't seen you in quite a while." He frowned and shook his head. "For that matter, I ain't seen very many people lately. Everybody seems to be staying at home these days." Then, smiling, he added, "Sho' am glad to see you, though. Now, tell me what I can do for you."

Katie handed Mr. Todd a list of supplies, which he quietly read. He pointed to the sign posted behind the counter: 'Can only take money for purchases. If you ain't got money, then anything that crows, cackles, moos, or oinks will do. No mules! '

Katie read the sign to Sadie. Sadie, still feeling slightly whimsical due to the unusually kind treatment these audacious gentlemen were bestowing upon her, giggled.

"I have something that oinks in the back of the wagon. Will that do?" Katie asked.

"If it's rooter and tooter is in good working condition, then I'll take it," laughed Mr. Todd.

Sadie and Katie smiled. Mr. McKinnon and his boys stood rigid and silent, afraid to make a response or to move. Katie relieved the tension when she winked and nodded at Mr. McKinnon. There was a sigh of welcome relief from the McKinnon clan. Soon, joyous laughter warmed the chill of the room where a dark cloud of gloom and fear had hovered.

Mr. McKinnon walked over to Katie and extended his hand. Graciously, she took the old codger's hand in hers. Momentarily, the two stood and looked deep into each other's eyes beyond the petty hurts and human fragility. A mutual respect, cast and bonded, would be the lasting terms of their relationship. Honesty was appreciated, trust was gained, and loyalty returned.

Once more, Mr. McKinnon tipped his hat to Sadie. Softly, he said, "Good day, ladies." Then he and his sons quietly left the store.

Sadie leaned towards Katie and whispered, "Like I said, this has been some kind of an amazing day."

Soon the McAllister wagon, loaded with supplies, headed down the street in the direction of McAllister's Lane. Just as Katie and Sadie approached the building that occupied Doc Owens's office, an old, familiar face spied them through the curtains of a front cased window. Years had etched his features, and shades of gray had grizzled his thinning hair. Profound as he was, he was extremely well thought of, generally as a caring and compassionate man. Doc Owens, overjoyed to see his old friends, called out through his opened door, "Katie! Sadie! Is that you?"

Katie jumped down from her wagon and scurried to him. They embraced as old-time, not-forgotten friends usually do. "Doc, am I glad to see you!"

"It's been a while. Thought you folks had moved from these parts." He looked up at Sadie sitting on the wagon seat and genially smiled. "Sure am glad you're back. There is no one in ten counties who can bake sweet cakes and apple pies like you, Sadie." Doc walked over to the beaming black lady and took her hand in his. "I am so sorry about what happened to Son. You and Jezra left before I had the chance to tell you."

Sadie bowed her head and nodded. As her heart filled with pain, she swallowed hard to hold back pooling tears.

Doc, after realizing those hurtful memories saddened Sadie, tried desperately to quickly change the subject. He whirled back to Katie. "Say, how's your papa? I heard that he has come home, too."

"He's doing fine, Doc."

"That's great news to hear. I'm glad that you folks are back where you belong." The old friend commented, "It has taken a lot of fortitude to overcome all the obstacles that your families have encountered. But you have won your battles. The McAllisters and the Kings."

"I feel like we have. It was a long, hard journey to get to that mountaintop. A lot of briars and brambles along the way, but we made it," Katie answered metaphorically.

"Well, you know that God didn't make any smooth mountains. Made all of 'em rocky so you can gleam from the climb. You people have always stood on a firm foundation. You've always leaned on your Maker to get you through the rough times. You know, there is a purpose to the events He places in our lives. Whether it's to make us laugh more or cry harder, He did promise to give us strength for the day. At first I was a bit concerned for you, Katie. I heard that you were so full of rage that several of 'em around here thought one of those scoundrels was surely going to die."

Doc was right. There had been a time when Katie did have a lot of anger in her heart. She did swear she would kill all the participants in Son's death. Nevertheless, she wanted her old friend to understand her long-fought-for transformation. Her face softened.

She slowly began, "For a while, I doubted that I would ever come to terms with what happened. But Papa told me that problems were a part of life."

"Your papa is a wise man."

"He also taught me that every person, regardless of color, faith, or status, was bound to have storms sooner or later. Just as the sun rises on the just and unjust, storms gather, too. It is the gathering storms that reveal to us the strengths of our faith. Knowing that God is the anchor gave me the faith to forgive all those who caused my and Sadie's family so much pain. He gave me such an inner peace when I finally trusted Him and let go of all that hate that I had built up inside of me. Somehow, Doc, there came a power in forgiveness. It was sort of freeing, if you know what I mean."

Doc, quite aware of Katie's strong character, always believed that her heart would one day be free from those chains of bitterness and shackles of hatred. He knew that she had found her anchor in the storm. Because Doc truly believed in Katie, his view concerning her character was never jaded.

At that moment, a rusty old pickup wheeled around to the front of Doc Owens's office. Ida Mae Buford jumped out from behind the driver's seat. Frantically, she scurried around the pickup to the other side. The door swung open on the passenger's side. Bent over and appearing to be in excruciating pain, Jackson Buford cried out when his wife attempted to lift him off the seat.

Quickly, Doc Owens hurried to his aid. "What's the matter with Jax, Ida Mae?"

"I don't know, Doc. He says that his midsection is hurtin' him bad."

"Lean back in the seat a minute, Jax, and let me see," ordered Doc.

Willingly, the man in severe pain obeyed.

Doc Owens lifted Jackson's shirt and pushed on his abdomen, causing an agonizing moan. "Help me get him inside to the examining table, Ida Mae."

The doctor carefully assisted Jax out of the pickup. With him leaning on them, Doc and Ida Mae carried Jax inside.

Katie noticed Sadie's tightly clenched hands holding her shawl. Gently, she squeezed Sadie's hands in an effort to show her concern and support. "Are you okay?" she asked tenderly.

For a moment, Sadie said nothing. Then she answered, "I will be. It's always hard for me the first time I see one of those men who dragged my boy away." Her eyes blurred as she quickly averted them from the sight of the once-despised man. With more assurance now, she lifted her chin proudly and added, "I'll be all right."

Katie smiled with admiration and unconditional love. "Sadie, do you know that you have already laid up enough bricks in Heaven to build a mansion?"

"Just like the one that Son is living in?"

"Just like Son." She climbed up on the wagon seat next to Sadie. "Let's go home. Our business here is done."

Just as Katie released the brake, Ida Mae ran out of the doctor's office.

"Katie! Wait!" she yelled. Ida Mae ran to the wagon. In a panic, she grabbed Katie's arm. "Please don't go! Doc says that Jax has the 'pendicitis. Says he got to operate." Tears began to flow as she continued to beseech Katie for help. "I can't help him do the drips to put my man asleep. Doc says that you are strong minded enough to do it for me."

Katie glanced at Sadie sitting stoically and staring straight ahead. Katie bit her lip as she contemplated what to do, not desiring to be of any help to the Bufords if it would upset Sadie. The decision was in Sadie's hands. Patiently, Katie waited for a response.

Suddenly, a tender smile softened Sadie's hardened face. "You go on inside and help the doc. I'll drive the wagon on home and put up our supplies."

Katie climbed down from the wagon. Once more, she hesitated as she looked questioningly up at Sadie.

Sadie winked. "Don't worry 'bout me. You go on in there and do what you can to help save that man's life. That's the right thing to do."

Yes, Sadie did have enough bricks laid up to build a mighty fine mansion, Katie thought.

"I'll see to it that Katie gets home," said Ida Mae. She looked up at the fragile black woman with pleading eyes that seemed to be begging for forgiveness. "Thank you, Sadie."

Katie and Ida Mae watched as Sadie rounded the corner and drove the wagon in the direction of McAllister's Lane.

"There goes a mighty fine woman," said Ida Mae.

"Yes ma'am. Not made any finer. She's full of compassion and all without measure."

From the door of Doc Owens's office, Katie and Ida Mae heard the pain-filled moans of Jackson Buford. As the women entered the two-room medical facility, Doc Owens called out for Katie. "Glad you stayed to help. Do you think that you can drip the chloroform in the mask?"

Katie confirmed with a nod.

Doc looked at Ida Mae. "Why don't you go on over to your sister's house for a visit? A long visit. I'll send for you just as soon as the operation is over and Jax is recovering."

Ida Mae, extremely edgy, willingly obeyed. It did not take much encouragement to persuade her to leave.

Katie followed Doc Owens into his office. On a dusty shelf sat an old, worn medical book. Doc took the book down from the shelf and brushed it off. Dust filled the air. Adjusting his spectacles so that he could read better, he thumbed through the pages until he found 'Appendicitis.' He glanced up at Katie. "Ain't done one of these in quite a while. Gonna have to read up a bit to refresh my memory."

"Whew," said Katie. "So that's what the doctors do when they tell you that they'll be back in a minute. They go sit in their office and read their medical books."

Doc chuckled. "Well, an ol' country doctor like me doesn't get much experience doctoring too many different things. Other than a soul being mule kicked, an occasional broke arm, and plenty of delivering newborns, this ol' doctor rarely gets to perform appendectomies and such. So I guess that I do have to refer to this old book once in a while."

A roguish grin crept across Katie's perky lips. "I sure do wish that I could tell Jax that you are in here reading up on how to cut his belly open and dig out his appendix. I bet that little bit of information would cause him to really make a big stink on that operating table."

Doc, a crusty old man and just as mischievous as Katie, looked up through his spectacles. "I don't remember the Hippocratic oath saying a thing about not taunting a man just before he goes under the drips...especially if he needed a good lesson taught to him."

Katie chuckled. "Doc, if you'll stay in here for about another five minutes reading that book, I'll fix it so that Ida Mae will have herself a mighty fine husband after his little surgery is over."

"Now, Katie, don't go shooting anything off like you did McKinnon's ear. Leave the man intact."

"Has he got a strong heart?"

"Strong as the smell of a mule's toot downwind."

"Five minutes, Doc, is all I need. I'm gonna make Jackson Buford as humble as Sadie's apple pies."

Doc looked up from his reading. Teasingly, he said, "Now, Katie, you're not going to hurt the man, are you?"

"Heck no, Doc. Only thing I'm gonna hurt is his feelings so that maybe he'll think twice next time he lets someone talk him into hanging an innocent boy."

Grinning, Doc shook his head. As Katie slipped out the door, he continued reading the surgical procedure for an appendectomy, unconcerned that Katie would do anything to harm his patient. He was well aware that Kathryn McAllister was a compassionate and caring person, except when someone was foolish enough to cross a McAllister or a King. Then, all havoc would break loose! Suddenly, that thought startled Doc. He looked up.

"Oh well, what the heck." He sighed and continued reading.

Leisurely, Katie strolled into the room where Jackson Buford was lying on the operating table. Moaning, Jax cocked an eye at Katie. Briefly, he contemplated his dire situation and made an unsuccessful attempt to get up.

"Hold on, Jax. Where do you think you're going?" asked Katie as she pushed him back down on the table. She leaned down close to Buford's face. His breath had a pungent smell of stale tobacco. Katie covered her nose. "Are all your finances in order, and have you laid all your sins down before the good Lord?"

"I'm getting out of here," growled Jax. He held tightly to his aching side. "Before you kill me." He blew air out of his mouth as a woman would do during labor. "Heard 'bout you shootin' McKinnon's ear off."

"He could have shot back." Katie's finger found Jax's tender spot on his aching side.

"Ouch! Doc! You know McKinnon can't hit a bear in the rear with a bass fiddle."

Katie turned her head to hide the naughty grin that she could not restrain from creeping across her face. Picking up one of the surgical knives lying on a table, she slowly ran her fingers down the blade, pretending to test it for sharpness.

Anxiously, Jax watched. Perspiration popped out on his face as he suspiciously eyed the razor-sharp surgical knife. Incredulously, he asked, "What ya gonna do with that?"

"Umm," replied Katie, "this knife is the one Doc is gonna open up your belly and gut you with."

Jax pulled his knees up into a fetal position and grabbed his sides. "Where's Doc?" He yelled much louder, "Doc!"

Katie made her next ploy when she picked up a stainless surgical pan. She held it up high so Jax could see. "And this pan is what I'm going to catch your guts in when they fall out of your belly!"

"Oh, help me, Lord," he moaned. "Why are you doing this to me?"

"Well, let me see. I guess because your lack of discernment has caused overwhelming emotional turmoil for me and the Kings, Jax," Katie said as she pretended to knick her finger on the knife. "Ouch!"

"Discernment? Heck, Katie, I don't even know what that word means."

"Oh, that's a new word I've just learned myself. See, I have this man and his family temporarily working for me on the farm." Katie walked around the table, occasionally prodding sensitive parts of Jax's body.

"That hurts!"

"He is quite the well-educated man. Went to some college, I think. Anyway, on our little breaks during the day, he teaches me. Words that I didn't know and things that I've never heard about… like history and science. You know, stuff like that."

"For whatever reason, why?" Jax managed to say through moans.

"I don't mind being a farm girl from the backwoods. I just don't want to be a *backward* farm girl from the backwoods."

At that moment, Doc Owens walked into the room.

"Doc, help me," Jax whispered. "Katie has gone crazy. She's fixin' to butcher me like some dang hog."

Doc Owens gently patted Jax's arm. "I am going to help you, son. I'm gonna help you get all better. Don't worry. Katie and I are going to take good care of you."

Jax groaned. He believed that death was imminent at the hands of Katie McAllister!

"Okay, Katie, let's begin to put ol' Jax to sleep," said Doc.

Katie walked over to the cabinet to get the chloroform and mask. While Doc turned to sterilize his instruments, Katie quietly eased back over to Jax's side. By this time, Jax was in too much pain to attempt to run.

Bending down, she whispered in his ear, close so he could hear, "Discernment means that you know you took a wrong turn in your life and you didn't have a care for the people you hurt. Your decision between right and wrong was not the best path to take, and now, Mr. Buford, whatever a man sows, he will also reap."

Jackson's eyes, wide with bewilderment, looked as if they would pop.

"I sure do hope that I don't make a mistake and not give you enough drops. It would be really a bad thing if you woke up in the middle of your surgery," Katie whispered as she made a gesture towards his abdomen. "You might wake up and see your guts in that pan."

Again Jax moaned, louder this time.

Katie added, "Just think, Jax. There were no chloroform drops for Son King. He felt *all* of his pain."

The last thing Jackson Buford thought about before he went under the anesthesia was whether or not he would actually wake up during his surgery. The thought of not ever waking up even crossed his mind!

Chapter 13

REDEMPTION'S CROSSROADS

The gears ground. Jackson Buford's rusty old pickup came to a stop at the end of the street. Ida Mae shifted the vehicle into first gear. Bumping along the dusty dirt road, hitting every pothole, Jax's wife turned toward McAllister's Lane. Katie sat quietly in the seat next to her.

Ida Mae was the first to speak. "You know, Katie, life is a little like this bumpy old road. Once you get over the bumps, the ridin' goes pretty smooth."

Katie remained motionless and speechless.

Ida Mae continued, "I want to thank you for helping Doc put Jax to sleep. I don't think that I would have been strong enough to do such as that."

Still, Katie remained silent and unyielding.

Further down the road, Ida Mae unrelentingly continued her conversation even though it appeared to be one-sided. "Katie, Jax is not a bad man. In my heart, I know that he is decent. Or at least halfway."

Ida Mae cast an indecipherable look towards Katie. Unconcerned, Katie's eyes remained fixed on the dusty road ahead.

"Jax was not himself that night they took Son," Ida Mae continued. "That stranger, the Western man, had him and all the others so liquored up, they would have followed him through a fire and then some."

The Western man? Suddenly, Katie's interest was spurred. Finally, she joined in the conversation with but one motive—to find out all she could about this stranger, the man who had incited the hanging. "Tell me what you know about this man."

"If I tell you all about it, will you promise not to say anything?" Ida Mae asked. "I'm not supposed to talk about it. Those were strict instructions from Jax."

Katie nodded. At this point, she would have agreed to anything to learn more about this mysterious stranger.

Ida Mae went on to say, "I don't know his name. Jax never would tell me that. But this man is part of the Ku Klux Klan."

Katie gasped. Ida Mae's words cut straight to her heart. She had heard about the Ku Klux Klan. This small but insidious growing group whose purpose was to instill a hatred of African-Americans and Jews, used murder and violence to evoke the intimidation of minorities. With the onset of the Depression, the group found an excuse to kindle its fires. The Klan used these vulnerable times as a perfect opportunity to further their cause. By blaming Blacks and Jews for the lack of jobs, family hardships, or any other adversities brought on by unemployment and a derailed economy, this notorious group threw the blame in the direction of minorities. The time was ripe for racial strife. They believed a white 'revolution' was the only 'solution.'

Ida Mae continued, "This man travels up and down the railroad tracks, from town to town. He stays for a while in a town that doesn't have an active organization of the Klan going on. From what I understand, his job is to organize chapters and find disgruntled Southern men to follow his cause of white supremacy."

The front wheels hit a washout in the middle of the road. The thrust caused by the bump in the road caused Ida Mae's and Katie's heads to hit the roof of the pickup. Katie's grip on the dashboard tightened, as did her jaw. Inside, her gut turned as her heart palpitated. Tears pooled. She was angry—bitterly angry.

Through clenched teeth, she smugly asked, "Is Jax mixed up with that cowardly bunch of sheet-wearing hoodlums? I thought that the people in our community agreed a long time ago to kiss off on those trouble-causing hypocrites."

The cohesive group of people who made up the small backwoods community in which Katie lived had long ago agreed on the fact that the races within their confines would be respected. This community, emboldened in God's potent presence, was permeated by the Spirit and enacted mercy and justice upon each individual man, woman, and child. What had caused these people to move so quickly to a lynching? Maybe racism was already there – only suppressed. Still, who had infected them with demonic capabilities, causing the good people of this community to forget their Christian commitments? There was only one answer. It was the stranger—the man who wore the bolo with the silver slide!

"Now, Katie, don't get upset. Of course, Jax is not a member of the Klan. All I was trying to tell you was that this fellow has been trying for some time now to get Jax and some others to form a chapter in this county."

Katie, angrier by the minute, demanded, "I want to hear everything."

"The day that Rosie O'Hara went missing, the stranger came around to our house. He had Whiskey Jones with him and a lot of Whiskey's 'shine. And he kept passing the jug around quite frequently."

"Tell me all you know."

"I could only hear bits and pieces of what he was saying, but he told Jax and the others that there needed to be an active group of Klan members in the county to keep the blacks in check. He said that sooner or later, a white girl or woman would end up being molested or perhaps murdered."

Katie grumbled, "So that was his plan of indoctrination."

Leaning towards Katie with a raised eyebrow, Ida Mae said, "The man told Jax and the others that if anything like that was to ever happen, the black people had to be taught a lesson…that the whites had to set an example by hanging the perpetrator… right then and there."

"But Son didn't kill Rosie. Son wouldn't hurt a flea," said Katie. Tears began to well in her soft, blue eyes. "If anyone had stopped long enough to ask questions, they could have found out the truth."

Ida Mae bit her lip and gripped the steering wheel tighter. Katie's words resonated. "Do you think that those men, including my Jax, helped to kill an innocent boy?"

"Yes."

Ida Mae glanced quickly at Katie. The pain she saw on her face saddened her. She took a deep breath as she tried to explain. "Everything just got so crazy that night. This stranger has a way about him. The things that he would say were so impressive. He could talk a bunch of men into doing anything for him." She sighed. "And the 'shine they were drinking didn't help them keep a straight head."

Katie wiped away a tear that gently fell. Her eyes narrowed when she replied, "It was an abomination! An evil invitation to corrupt our community's beliefs. It was useless. It was cruel." The images of that violent night returned.

"Yes, it was cruel," agreed Ida Mae. "It was a mistake. A terrible mistake. But Katie, please don't be bitter toward your neighbors and friends for the rest of your life. And believe it or not, something good always comes from the mistakes people make. You've got to believe that, and you've got to believe that all of us are truly sorry."

Tears continued to blur Katie's eyes. "I don't have any hatred or bitterness in my heart for Jax, Buster Reese, or the McKinnons.

Or any of the others who were there that night. I dealt with that issue some time ago. On the other hand, this stranger is a horse of a different color. I'll see him again. One day. And when I do, I will make him pay." Her tone was confident yet harsh. "He will pay. I swear it on Son's life."

For a fleeting moment, chills ran down Ida Mae's spine. Katie's icy glare caused her to shiver. Just as she passed the O'Haras' place and turned the old pickup onto McAllister's Lane, Ida Mae glanced over her shoulder to the spot where Son had died. Remnants of the charred stump of the Judgment Tree remained standing as a reminder of racial injustice.

Katie remembered well the faces of all the men who were at the hanging that dreadful night. Other than Creel Burr's, one other person stood out—the stranger dressed in Western wear with a silver clasp on a string necktie.

"One more question, Ida Mae," said Katie. "This man whom we've been talking about…was he wearing a string necktie with a silver clasp?"

For a moment, there was a brief silence in the pickup. Unflinchingly, Ida Mae answered a definite "yes."

Katie's cold glares turned into restless agitation. Slowly and more confident now, she turned to Ida Mae. For a brief moment, their eyes locked. "Woe be to this man with the silver clasp. Woe be to this man who I am going to make stand accountable. Katie McAllister is going to send this man to Satan's Hell!"

The road to redemption had been long, from a deep-seated hatred to a forgiving spirit freeing the soul from the ill will harbored deep within her heart. It was a daily struggle not to be controlled by a carnal mind. Once again, Katie found herself at redemption's crossroads. Would she trust in her salvation, or would she allow herself to live continuously in a way that brought retribution with no peace? Would she accept or would she resent? Trust or never let go? Only time would tell.

And the gears ground.

Chapter 14

TREASURED LEGACY

*D*raws from the sweet potato had taken root in the rich, loamy South Georgia soil. Lush green vines, burgeoning with new growth and perkily displaying their delicate heads, danced in the breeze caused by a gentle wind. Sweet fragrances of the greening plants moved along by the gentle breeze under a deep blue sky. William Hampton inhaled. The sweet air permeated his lungs.

William and Katie stood at the field's edge, admiring God's handiwork. The bounty of the land and fruits of their labor were good. Made sore by the handles of the plow irons, their hands ached. Nonetheless, they were pleased with their accomplishments.

William looked across the field to the towering ancient hardwoods. Growing up in a city, he knew he was a long way from the ordinary. "I never knew that the living in the country would be like this," he whispered, careful not to disturb the solitude of the moment.

Amidst the bucolic scene was peacefulness; it was calm yet awe-inspiring. In the distance, the song of meadowlarks and the frantic call of the killdeer interrupted the sound of the wind whistling through the trees. Occasionally, a bobwhite would call out for his mate. The air was filled with the melodious music of the crickets and cicadas strumming their motors, whirling their symphony through the crisp, clean air.

Katie, squatting on the ground, slowly stood. "There's no other place I'd rather be. I guess that I'm a little prejudiced, but I wouldn't live anywhere else. Papa says that I'm a true daughter of the soil, and the land is in my blood."

"A true-to-heart farm girl, huh?" said William.

"Most definitely."

Yet again, William dreamily gazed out across the land proliferating with the grandeur of God's creation. "It takes my breath away."

Katie smiled. She, too, enjoyed the splendor of the earth that lay before them. In a softer tone, she added, "In the spring, the woods come alive with new growth after sleeping all winter. When autumn slips in, it's like a faint whisper sliding across an artist's palette." A soft chuckle gurgled in her throat. Her pensive eyes gazed over the land. "It's like Mother Nature takes out her paintbrush and splashes color all about like one of Sadie's patchwork quilts, like the one she uses to spread over me on cool nights. Just like Sadie, the greatest mother of all, spreads her quilt of colors over McAllister's Lane. I stand humbled and in awe. This place is our treasured legacy. Our roots grow deep. McAllister's Lane is my home and forever will be," said Katie.

Katie and William lingered, listening to the sound of the clinking of the old windmill. In the distance, they watched the ethereal beauty and fragile grace of a white-tailed deer as she loped across the meadow.

"I never realized that there is a good side to farm life and to those who work the soil." William sighed. "City life is so complicated, but the country has an ease and pace of its own. Unblemished. Perfected but untamed."

Katie laughed. "Are you saying that country folks are a little wild?"

William reciprocated her jest. "Heck no, Kat. Just the opposite. People are so easygoing here. Relaxed. When you drive down the road, the person you meet stops and speaks to you. You end up chatting for hours with someone who you don't even know. Everyday things that I always took for granted seem to be genuine in the backwoods. Life is good here."

William stopped momentarily as he watched a butterfly falling from the sky, stopping to rest and feast on a nearby honeysuckle. He shook his head. "I guess you think that I'm a little overblown in my opinion of country versus city?"

"No, I think that you're a man who just appreciates the simple life." Katie grinned. "And you are always welcome here. Just don't try to change us."

"No, no. Not ever. Katie, I'll tell you one thing that I've learned since I've lived here. It's not the material things you have in your life but *who* you have in your life that really count."

William knew that he had earned Katie's respect. In return, a mutual trust and loyalty were gained between them. He turned to face his newfound friend. "Ann, the children, and I don't have to leave right now. We can stay on for a while. To tell you the truth, I'd like to see this crop through."

Katie laughed. "You get a little dirt under your fingernails and it's seeping through to your veins, huh? Are you becoming a man of the soil?"

William returned the sentiment. "You know, Kat, I never thought that I would say this, but I really enjoy working on a farm. I love the fresh, clean air and the scent of the dirt and the feel of it in my hands." He pointed to the small plants. "And I get a lot of pleasure out of watching them take root in the earth and grow into something productive and good."

"Jezra says that roots are the bones of the earth. They hold the earth together and keep it from slipping apart. He says if the dirt has roots, then it is good earth. Not like deserts with shifting sands."

"Jezra is a wise man."

"That he is."

"The children love him and Sadie. They love you, too. And Ann is finally learning how to cook!" William joked.

They stood breathing in the fragrant breeze of the greening sod as the wind whispered. The warm sunlight penetrated their bodies. From the field's edge, a raccoon moved silently across the field.

William reiterated, almost pleading, "It's so peaceful. I really hate to leave."

Katie turned to him. She explained, "I'm sorry, William. I wish I could keep you and your family here. I do understand how you feel, but since the decline in the economy it's hard enough for me and Papa to feed ourselves without adding four extra mouths. I truly wish that there was a way, but I just don't see how."

William turned to Katie and extended a grateful hand. For a moment, Katie gazed sympathetically into William's eyes. She completely understood his sentiments about living in the country. She also understood his apprehension about continuing his journey to Birmingham. Traveling with a family, especially riding the rails, was not exactly safe these days.

"I'm going to miss you, Katie."

"I will miss you, too. Just remember that real friendships last forever."

"I know. Hopefully, our paths will cross many times."

"I am sure they will."

Katie took both of William's hands in hers. His hands had become rough and calloused over the past weeks. She opened them, palms up. "These are good hands, William Hampton. They are not afraid of hard work, and yet they know how to be gentle and kind to a wife and children." She lifted her eyes to meet William's. "One of these days, these hands are going to do great and wonderful things." Katie chuckled as she remembered the first day they had met when William was making a futile attempt to butcher a cow. "Maybe you'll be a doctor one day."

He reciprocated her humor. "Just not a surgeon!"

Katie laughed and for a moment became silent. Finally, she spoke. "In my short life, I have learned that life is all about how we look at ourselves. The greatest challenge is being happy with what you find once you've figured out who you are. Yes, it's going to be an honor for me to say that I knew you. One day, you are going to finish your education and make a fine doctor."

William smiled. He was at a loss for words. Over the last few months, he had grown to admire Katie for her courage and her sense of honesty and fairness. She always gave without expectation and never asked for anything in return. She was as constant as the moon and the stars, always there and always to be counted on. He would miss her greatly.

With a bowed head, he softly added, "You know, Kat, you not only came into my life for a season, but you will always remain in my heart. I am so thankful that our friendship will last longer than a season. It will last a lifetime."

For a long while, the two friends stood at the field's edge, not talking but simply enjoying each other's companionship. They would greatly miss one another.

"Tomorrow, I'll take you and your family to Albany to a freight yard to jump a train. Albany is a railroad connector. Trains move in and out from all directions. We'll find one that will take you to Birmingham. Besides, it's much easier to jump a train there with children. It will be easier for them to climb on a train that's not moving."

"What will they do with us if they catch us?"

"Generally, nothing. The people who work in the railroad yards are always willing to look away, especially if they see a couple with children getting on a boxcar. They understand that families who 'hobo' have somewhere they need to go and no money to get there." Much sadder now, Katie added, "Sadie will pack you enough food to last you for a long time. Just remember not to get off the train until you get to Birmingham, and please don't steal anyone's cows." She managed a chuckle this time. "The next person you steal from might not be so generous."

William took his handkerchief out of his back pocket and knelt down on one knee. With his hands, he scooped up a pile of soft, brown dirt. Placing the dirt inside his handkerchief, he tied it securely to keep any from spilling. Slowly, he rose and held his small package of dirt out for Katie to see.

"I'm taking a little piece of McAllister's Lane with me," he said. Blinking back tears from stinging eyes, he once again gazed across the sea of green against a blue sky. "To remember." As he brushed the soil from his hands, he whispered, "And I will always hold a place in my heart for Katie McAllister."

The next morning, the Hamptons piled in the 1925 Ford pickup that had been stored in the barn for some time. Since they had reconciled themselves to leaving McAllister's Lane, they now anxiously waited to continue their journey.

Sadie handed Ann a basket of food. "Now, don't let none go to waste, but don't eat it all at once. And don't let Katie forget to go by Mr. Thoms's livery barn to get my mama's shawl. Remind her that I left it hanging on a nail in the loft where me and Jezra slept."

William shook Jezra's and Thomas's hands. "Take care, now, and don't be taking in any more strangers," he teased. "Sure you don't want to ride along?"

"Nope. Don't have nothing I want to go back to see. Besides, Jezra and I have got to butcher that ol' cow that broke her leg." Thomas smiled. "Don't worry none. Katie will get you there safe and sound."

As William Hampton watched Katie walking towards the pickup, he pondered on this controversial lady of the soil. Casting a quizzical look towards Thomas, he inquired, "I want to ask you something. That girl is like nobody else I have ever met in my life. She is tolerable yet fair. Predictable but unconventional. Yet on the day she caught me butchering your cow, I was terrified. Do you think, Thomas, that Katie would have really hanged me?"

Thomas laughed as he pointed towards his daughter. "William Hampton, that girl is one of the fairest, most honest, most forgiving people you'll ever have the pleasure to meet. She has compassion and a deep concern for others. No sir, she would not bring any harm to you or your family." Thomas cocked one eye and looked over at William. Mischievously, he grinned. "Unless she thought for one minute that you would do something to hurt any of us. Then she would hang your hide across a tree limb by the neck. And she would leave you there to rot!"

William Hampton gulped as he ran his finger around the edge of his collar.

"What are you two conspiring about now?" asked Katie as she ambled to the truck.

"Aw, nothing," Thomas said, winking at William. "Just saying I hope you have enough gas to get there and back."

The drive to Albany took much longer than Katie had anticipated. She drove extra slowly to conserve gasoline, a valued commodity during the Depression.

Finally, they arrived at the Broad Street bridge. Katie stopped in the middle of the bridge to allow the Hamptons to view the gentle, flowing waters of the Flint, a place of permanence in Katie's mind. Sweeping low branches bowed from the riverbanks like long, graceful fingers of a fine and delicate southern lady. Spanish moss hung from the limbs, flimsily dragging through the steady current.

Katie said, "Hundreds of years ago, a tribe of Creek Indians lived at the river's edge in houses made out of sticks and mud."

"Wow! Really?" asked William.

"Yes and they called the river Thronateeska."

"Thronateeska? Do you know what it means?"

Katie dreamily gazed at the river, imagining a young brave chipping away at a flint rock. "A place where the flint is picked up."

Before she shifted into gear, she forced herself to look towards the other side of the river in the direction of the train trestle—the place where Creel Burr had died. Somehow, it seemed like ages ago that she had witnessed the old hobo throwing himself in the path of an oncoming train.

William asked, "What are you in such deep thought about, Katie?"

Katie hesitated before answering William. "I was just thinking that life is a lot like this river. As the waters move downstream, you never touch the same water twice."

"You said that one day you would tell me about what happened at the river's edge."

Katie decided to allow the past to die along with Creel and Son. "It's a long story," she said, "one that I'd rather forget than remember. If it's okay with you, let it die."

William nodded. He respected her discretion.

At the railroad yard, farewells were difficult for William, for his family, and for Katie as well. The Hamptons and McAllisters had grown close during their stay together on the farm. It was best that they say as little as possible since good-byes were already hard enough.

As soon as the yardman looked away, William Hampton and his family made a quick dart for the empty boxcar at the railroad terminal. Katie watched as William boosted his family aboard just in time before the yardman turned back around. They hurriedly scampered to the back of the boxcar and crouched in a corner before being seen.

Within a few minutes, the engineer pushed forward on the throttle of the great steel engine. Gradually, it began to chug down the track. The creaking and groaning of the swaying cars and the soft puffing of the steam pistons finally disappeared. The Hamptons were gone. Katie's heart was heavy. Deep inside, there was emptiness.

Turning her attention to the matters at hand, Katie started for Mr. Thoms's barn, as promised, to retrieve Sadie's shawl, which meant so much to her. Suddenly, something inside compelled her to turn the truck in another direction. Without knowing or understanding why, she found herself heading for the train trestle, the place where Creel Burr had died.

Soon she was there. For a while, she stared at the place where Creel had camped that night. She reminisced about his confessing that he was the one who had killed Rosie O'Hara. She had tried to understand him for what he was—a man on the prowl, always looking for his prey. He was a man who rode the rails and searched for victims to maintain his control and power. Memories came flooding back of a lone train whistle and Creel propelling himself backwards onto the tracks as the steel engine approached. She trembled, remembering the lingering images of that tragic event.

Softly, her own words pelted her eardrums. "Creel, I don't know where you are right now, but I'm pretty sure that you are not singing with the angels."

Katie turned the truck in the direction of Mr. Thoms's barn. Abruptly, she stopped. Slowly and deliberately, she turned around in the seat. "But there is one thing I do know for sure, Creel. Soon, a man who is wearing a silver bolo slide will be joining you."

Chapter 15

LEADER OF ILL REPUTE

Memories flooded Katie's soul like the slow-moving currents of the Flint River as the pickup chugged towards Mr. Thoms's livestock barn, the place where Thomas and then Jezra once worked. Clouds gathered as a dark, dismal sky developed. A chilling, blustery wind began to stir. Katie pulled up the collar on her shirt to cut the brisk wind, sending chills down her neck. As she drove up to the livestock barn, she stopped and looked for signs of Mr. Thoms's whereabouts. However, there was no indication that anyone was present. Instead, an unusual quietness and stillness surrounded the place. No mules brayed, and no horses whinnied. An unlatched hayloft door slamming against the wall of the barn as the wind gusted was the only noise.

Anxiously, Katie eased out of the truck and walked inside the barn. Towards the rear, seated on a bale of hay and leaning against a post, was a rather tall, burly man much in need of a shave and a haircut. Scraggy stubble encased a solid jaw. A brown jug he held in his hand emitted a strong odor, reeking of whiskey. Startled, the man glared at Katie through red, swollen eyes. "Who are you?"

"I'm Katie McAllister. I'm looking for the owner, Mr. Thoms." She glanced around the barn for the man who was revered by her father and Jezra.

The tall, brawny man stood, staggering due to the ill effects of the whiskey. He grabbed the post to hold himself steady. "The old coot died a while back."

Katie took a deep breath. Slowly, she exhaled. "Now what?" she said more to herself than to the intoxicated stranger.

The man continued, "Keeled over with a heart attack." He attempted to point to one of the stalls. "Right over there."

"I'm sorry," said Katie. "My father said that he was a good man."

"Yeah. He was."

There was a silence in the place; the quietness was eerie. Finally, Katie spoke. "Who owns this place now? I need to talk to the owner about getting a friend's shawl. Her husband worked here for a while. Mr. Thoms allowed them to sleep in the loft. Sadie, my friend, said that her shawl should be hanging on a nail up there." Katie motioned, pointing towards the loft.

The tall man cleared his filmy throat and spit. "Reckon that'll be me. My pa was the owner. He left me this place." Bloodshot, puffy eyes ravenously traced the outline of Katie's shapely body.

He spoke again. "I know who you are. Your pa and the Kings used to talk about you all the time." A voracious grin spread across his dirty, stubbly face. "But they never told me that Katie McAllister was such a fine-looking woman."

Slowly, Katie eased her way towards the entrance of the barn. The repugnant drunk woved his way to the big doors, following her with enchanted eyes. "You can go up in the loft and get that shawl anytime," he sneered with a sly laugh. "And if there's anything else I can do for you, just let me know."

Katie responded to his remark as a direct offense to her integrity and character. She froze and then wheeled around to face the rude man. "You know, it's a pity," she began.

"What's that?"

"From what I have heard about your father, he was a good and kind man," continued Katie. "It's sad that somebody as loathsome as you came from his loins."

The drunk man was startled by Katie's insolent remark. Her words stung and were quite sobering. "I'm sorry," he slurred. "I guess that I am pretty loathsome. Would you accept my apology?"

Pointing to the liquor jug that the man was holding, Katie remarked, "I know it was the booze talking. You need to stop drinking that stuff. You know, nothing but no good ever comes from that, and in the end, it never solves your problems."

Mr. Thoms's son laid the brown jug down on the ground and, with awe and admiration, watched Katie McAllister walk away.

Outside, the gathering storm caused the sky to rumble. Suddenly, pelting rain dropped violently in a downpour. Katie covered her head and scurried for the pickup, leaving the drunken man standing at the door. In just a short while, he too ran to his own truck and drove off through the rainstorm, weaving as he spun away into the dreary night.

For a while, Katie watched as he disappeared down the road. The rain was intense with visibility extremely limited as huge drops pounded the vehicle. Finally, she decided that driving in this rainstorm was too dangerous. Patiently, she waited for the rain to end.

An hour passed, then two. As darkness settled, it was evident that there was no relief from the torrential downpour. It appeared that it would be best if she stayed the night. But where? The dry barn and the smell of fresh hay in the loft came to mind—a good place for her to bed down. Her plan was to rise early and slip out before Mr. Thoms's son returned. Little did she know that bedding down in a soft, warm place for the night would be the last thing she would do.

Katie parked the pickup in a well-hidden place; then, covering her head, she scampered back to the barn. Pushing the door closed, she turned to look for the ladder leading to the loft. After shaking off as much water as she could, she slowly ascended into the hayloft. At the top of the ladder, she stopped. Looking around, she spied Sadie's shawl still hanging on a nail.

Bedding down in the soft, fragrant hay, Katie listened to the muttering of the pigeons high in the rafters and the wind whistling through the cracks and around the corners of the barn. Suddenly, she heard a rumble of pickups screeching to a halt outside the barn. The sound of the truck doors slamming was sharp and clear. One of the barn's side doors was slung open. A dozen strange men came running inside out of the rain, stomping the mud off their boots and shaking the rainwater from their coats and hats.

As quietly as she could, Katie eased to the back of the loft and hid behind a pile of hay. On her belly, she gazed through a small crack in the loft floor. Below was a group of men gathering around their leader. Self-righteous and arrogant, he stood on a bale of hay so that he could be seen above the group. The small band of followers was mesmerized by his every word. Katie scanned the small crowd, enthralled by the person in charge, who was fully in control.

Abruptly, she froze! She immediately rolled onto her back, quickly covering her mouth to smother sobbing gasps. Her heart was pounding; her head was reeling. She could hardly believe what her eyes had seen. Quietly, she rolled over and once more glared through the crack in the floor of the loft. Yes! She was right! The man standing on the bale of hay was wearing a necktie with a silver bolo slide. It was the Klansman from Texas!

"If we don't take this country back from black people and Jews," the man with the silver slide yelled, "there won't be any jobs left for the white man!"

His captivated audience applauded. Swelling words from this man with a great oratorical gift held his small audience spellbound.

The agenda was simple—suppress minorities by instilling fear. Clenched fists shook vehemently. Smooth-tongued, beguiling, deceiving promises of a better life for those who followed him drove his point cleverly into the heart of each man.

"Jobs are too scarce as it is. And if we don't start making examples out of some of these people around here, the white man is not going be able to feed and take care of his own family. We'll use whatever methods we have — ropes, guns, and fire — to terrorize those people and take back what belongs to us."

His followers, enemies of justice, mirrored the ideals of their leader with whom they agreed. "Yeah! Yeah!" They cheered, clapped their hands, and shook their fists.

The pious leader hurled blasphemous accusations to those who objected to his cause. A sharp, pointed tongue spurred deceptive words as he vehemently laid out his plans. "Just as soon as this rain stops, we're driving to that small community outside of this town, and we're going to burn down that church where the black preacher man keeps preaching to his congregation to work hard in those cotton fields. Work hard in the mills. Work hard so the white boss will hire you and not hire the whites. We will not stand for it! Do you agree? The white knights will torch that church! Tonight!"

The church was the center of the Black society. Burning their churches suppressed them even further by instilling fear in blacks and exploiting hatred in whites. The mysterious traditions of devious and murderous acts of the sheet-wearing members of the Klan invoked terror, violence, and intimidation.

Groans came from the enraged group, held spellbound under the deceptive influence of the man with the silver slide.

The man shook his fists even harder as his tone bellowed above the applause. "We will put food on the table for our families. We will take back our jobs. And we will take back our country! Hail to whites!"

They echoed, "Hail to whites!"

The men, emotions intensified by their leader with the string necktie and the silver slide, were ready to accept his evil invitation and follow the heathen down a path of abomination and sin. Willingly, they submitted to his manipulative authority. Enslaved by his words and drawn in by his schemes, they would obey his voice and fall into the defilement of executing acts of violence.

Katie leaned against the wall of the barn. So this is how he was able to get good, honest men to do his dirty work. His tongue was like the tips of his boots—pointedly sharp!

Slowly, she crawled to the loft window. Looking below, she noticed a rope secured around a pulley that could perhaps hold her weight. Just as she reached for the rope, a hand reached out from behind her! The strong grip grasped her mouth tightly, smothering a scream. An even stronger arm pulled Katie backwards, forcing her down into the hay. Coal-black eyes looked deep into her soft blue ones. She held her breath, too frightened to breathe.

A young, handsome man about her age placed his finger over his mouth. "Shhh," he whispered. "Don't go that way. The pulley is loose. You'll fall for sure and might bust that pretty little..." He stopped. By the looks of this wildcat he was trying to hold still, he thought it best not to finish his sentence.

The young man's hair was dark and wavy. Broad shoulders topped his medium frame. A soft, tender smile crossed his lips. In that moment, the sight of him astounded Katie, stealing her very breath.

Unexpectedly, the wind caught the loft window, blowing it against the side of the barn. A loud crashing noise ensued. Pigeons frantically , flapping their wings made their escape through the open window. Below, the men looked up toward the loft, startled. The leader from Texas motioned with a quick nod of his head. One of his followers gallantly obeyed and began to climb the ladder, looking for the origin of the mysterious noise.

Quickly, the young, handsome man reached out for Katie's hand and quietly led her to the other side of the loft. Willingly, she followed. For some reason, one she could not explain, she trusted him. In fact, foremost in her mind, she could sense that he was a man of good deeds—honorable and true. Together, they concealed themselves under a deep pile of loose hay. Quietly, they waited.

The man sent up to inspect the loft carefully scanned the surroundings. Once again, the force of the wind caused the window to slam against the barn wall. Satisfied that the wind was the source of the noise, he walked over to the window and secured it with a rope.

"It's just the wind!" the man yelled down to the others, who anxiously waited.

Katie and the young man remained silent and still, well hidden under the hay.

The man walked cautiously back to the loft ladder. Just as he started to step down, he noticed Sadie's shawl lying in the hay.

"Huh," he chuckled. "That ol' boy Thoms must have had something going on up here."

Once more, he started his descent. Almost within the same second, a pitchfork fell over from the side of the loft where Katie and the young man were hidden. The man hesitated and then stepped back up into the loft. His eyes darted from side to side, searching. Slowly and carefully, he crept towards the fallen pitchfork.

The men below listened; they waited.

The handsome young man pulled Katie closer. She could feel his breath on her face. She held hers.

Suddenly, an old tomcat jumped down from the rafters, meowed, and scampered away. Relieved, the man let out a "whew."

Although somewhat satisfied that the cat was the culprit that caused the pitchfork to fall, the man again briefly scanned the area. Satisfied, he indicated to the others that no one was there.

A brown jug filled with liquor was being freely passed around to the repugnant group below. More incensed with each passing of the intoxicating beverage, they became louder and more indignant.

Satisfied that all was well, the young man holding Katie began to stir. As he brushed the hay from her face, he gently pulled a straw tangled in her blond hair. He pulled her close. Katie's heart was beating so loudly, she thought that he would surely hear. He leaned towards her and softly whispered in her ear, "They'll be leaving soon. Stay here and be quiet. You'll be safe." He put his finger over his lips to signal her to remain silent.

As the young man turned to go, Katie grabbed his arm and pulled him back on the hay near her. She whispered in his ear, "Where did you come from? How did you get here?"

"Whoa, now. One question at a time. I was here before you climbed your prissy pants up here and I suppose I came up to this loft for the same reason you did."

"What do you mean?"

"I mean, to get out of the rain!"

"Shh… lower your voice!"

"Lower my voice? You're the one yelling!"

Katie continued with her questioning. "Where were you? I didn't see anyone here when I climbed up."

"That's because I was hiding from you, sassy pants!"

"Prissy? Sassy? Which one am I?"

The young man gave a sensual glance at the pants Katie was wearing. "Well, maybe a little of both."

The young man lowered his voice. "I'd like to stay around and talk some more but that black preacher they're going to visit tonight is a friend of my papa. I'm going to warn him that the Klan is coming to burn down his church."

He turned to go but suddenly changed his mind and turned to face Katie. Putting his lips to her ear, he whispered, "By the way, it's been a pleasure meeting you, ma'am."

Carefully, he untied the rope that held the window. The wind had stopped blowing, but he secured it just in case. Beside the window was a wooden ladder nailed to the outside of the barn. Slowly, he descended. Crouching, he dashed across the barnyard to his pickup, which was well hidden behind some trees. From a moment, he hesitated, wondering if he did the right thing by leaving that girl inside. "Oh well," he murmured. Just as he started the engine, Katie slipped onto the seat beside him.

The young man jumped. Katie's sudden appearance startled him. "What are you doing?" he asked.

"I slipped down the ladder right after you did. I'm going with you."

"No, ma'am, you are not!" he sternly barked.

"Look, there are ten men inside that barn and only one of you. Don't you think that you're a little outnumbered?"

He chuckled. "Not really. I may look it, but I'm not stupid. All I'm going to do is warn Preacher Smith that the Klan is coming so he'll have time to get his family to safety. I don't have any intention of getting in any type of confrontation with that group. This dog don't fight!"

"Look, whatever your name is…"

"John Luke McCoy. Call me Luke."

"Well, Luke, I happen to know the man in that barn who's getting those men riled. And he has more on his agenda than just burning a cross and burning down a church. He takes it all the way. Your Preacher Smith will either end up hanged or burned alive."

Luke frowned. He did not know this girl with the soft skin and blue eyes, but for some reason, he felt inclined to listen to her. "What can just the two of us do to stop them?"

Katie pointed to her pickup that she had parked on the side of the barn. "I've got a Henry rifle under the seat."

Luke added, "And I have a shotgun in here."

She smiled. "Well, Luke McCoy, as I see it, that's all we'll need for now."

Katie slid out of the pickup and maneuvered over to her vehicle. As quietly as she could, she opened the door and eased her rifle out from under the seat. Then, just as quietly, she closed the door. Momentarily, she stopped behind one of the Klan member's pickups parked near hers. As she lifted her head to look around, she noticed that in the truck bed was a rope and an ax. She quickly extracted them. Another glance inside the cab gave her the idea of snatching other useful items. With her newly acquired arsenal, she crouched low and darted back to Luke's pickup.

She laid them in the bed and through the window whispered to Luke, "I think that the owner of that pickup over there makes a little moonshine on the sly. There's a whole sack of sugar lying in his front seat, and I don't think he's gonna use it to sweeten his tea."

"So what? If you are going with me, you'd better get in and lets go, or else, this boy is fixing to ride!"

"Hold on a minute. He's got something else in that truck that might can be used to slow 'em down."

Before Luke could respond, Katie was scampering back to the Klansman's truck. Also inside was a sack of potatoes. Luke watched intently, wondering what she was going to do.

Quietly, she opened the door and took out a few potatoes. Just as she started to leave, she saw something else of interest lying on the floorboard—white hoods worn by the Klansmen. Katie could not resist. She picked them up and promptly stuffed them inside her shirt.

"Never know if these will come in handy."

Luke, strained his eyes to watch Katie. Indeed, this woman was a curiosity.

Suddenly, one of the members of the Klan opened the barn door and stepped outside, checking to see if the rain had ceased. Luke lay down in the seat. Katie quickly ducked behind the back of the pickup. The Klansman held out his hand to catch raindrops. Satisfied that the rain had cleared, he went back in to tell the others.

Katie was not deterred. More determined than ever to accomplish her mission,

Luke, peering over the steering wheel, said, "What the…?"

Katie shoved as many potatoes as she could into the exhaust pipe. Then she scooped up mud and packed it in with the potatoes. Katie scurried back to Luke's truck. Out of breath, she jumped on the seat beside him. "You'd better take off like a scalded cat with running gears. They'll be coming out of that barn soon now that it's stopped raining."

Luke put the pickup in gear and smashed the accelerator. Down the road they sped, straight for the small community where Preacher Smith lived. A few miles later, Luke, still nervous over the close encounter back at the barn, asked Katie, "I'd like to ask you one question. Why did you steal that man's potatoes and then stuff them with mud in that man's exhaust pipe?"

Katie looked at him with a cocked eye. "I didn't steal his potatoes. They're in the truck."

"Yeah, in the exhaust pipe!"

"Well, you see, God helps those who help themselves. I just helped myself to his potatoes so God could help us lessen the odds, of course. I simply blocked the exhaust pipe so that the fumes will back up and suffocate the engine." She winked.

Frowning, Luke glanced at the beautiful woman sitting by his side. Somehow, he knew that knowing her would be the beginning of an eternally fruitful life. Little did he know that he was heading for an amazing journey.

Katie smiled. "One truck down and three to go."

"That seems to be an awfully hard thing to do to somebody."

Her impatience began to show. "I take it that you haven't had any dealings with the Klan," she said abruptly. "The Klan is a worthless waste of God-given energy." She was anything but humble with her reply. "What I did to his truck doesn't bother me one minute. Lucky for him, that's all I'm going to do."

"Oh."

"So, Mr. McCoy, you'd better drive like two bulldogs stuck in a washtub. We need to get to Preacher Smith in a hurry. The intentions of those men we left back there at the barn won't hold a candle to what I did to that truck."

With raised eyebrows, Luke glanced over towards Katie. Sternly, she gazed straight ahead. Without saying another word, Luke stomped the accelerator down even harder, straight to Preacher Smith and the community where he lived. Like two bulldogs stuck in a washtub!

Chapter 16

THE CARPENTER'S PLAN

*S*trong fists pounded the wood-framed door of Willy Smith's small shanty. Soon a sleepy-eyed old man opened the door in response to the hard, furious pummeling. The black preacher was smaller in stature than Katie. He put his spectacles on and strained to see the faces of his night visitors. Holding a lantern up to get a closer look, he stared questioningly into the frantic eyes of Luke McCoy and Katie McAllister.

"Can I help you, young people?"

"Mr. Willy, don't you recognize me?" asked Luke.

Preacher Willy Smith strained his eyes harder to see the face of the persistent young man. "Oh yeah, you'd be Luther McCoy's boy. Yeah, I know your pa. What be the problem, boy?"

"Preacher Smith," began Luke, "as we speak, the Klan is coming here tonight to burn your church to the ground." More desperate sounding now, Luke continued, "You have to get your family and everyone else in this community to safety. Get them out of bed, Preacher Smith, and hide them in the woods. Now!"

In the small black community, there was a row of shanties beside the house of Preacher Willy Smith. Mr. Lester Cartwright, a carpenter, lived next door to the preacher. Next door to him was Jeremiah Odum, the beekeeper. On down the lane were two families with whom Luke was not familiar. The last house on the lane belonged to Snake. Snake, a homeless orphan who could not speak, had wandered into the community when he was in his mid-teens. A long scar on his neck indicated an injury to his voice box. Strange as it seemed, Snake had acquired his name because he took a liking to eerie, crawling reptiles. In his house, he had snakes of all kinds, including rattlers. Although he kept his pets in boxes, his neighbors were afraid to enter the house. At the very end of the lane was the community church the Klan had planned to burn to the ground.

Preacher Smith hurriedly put on his pants over his faded nightshirt. He gathered his frightened family and rushed them into the woods to hide. An aging wife, two daughters, and three grandchildren scurried to the safety of the confines of the wooded area behind their home. Then Preacher Smith, along with Luke and Katie, hastily knocked on the doors of the other families, hustling them off out of sight. Everyone had gathered what could be carried in his or her arms and quietly exited their homes to a safe secret place. The small children and babies were hushed as they moved into the darkness and the safety of the big trees and underbrush.

Everyone went to hide except for Mr. Cartwright, the carpenter, and Mr. Odum, the beekeeper. They staunchly refused to leave, determined to remain and fight for their homes. Although Luke and Katie repeatedly urged the men to go, the pair soon realized that their pleading was useless. These men had invested their lives in their homes and would not run. Instead, they would stand their ground.

Luke was left with no other choice but to remain and assist with their fight. He indicated to the others that they must quickly devise a plan. He suggested, "We have to come up with a plan and fast. The Klan is probably less than an hour behind us. They have more men and, consequently, more guns." He asked, "Does anyone have any ideas?"

Mr. Cartwright, the carpenter, replied, "I know how to slow 'em down." The group eagerly waited for him to share his plan. "Help me take the doors and shutters off my house. We can hammer nails on the underside and lay them across the road down where the road bends. When their pickups run over those boards, the nails will puncture their tires." He smiled as he noticed that everyone was in agreement. "That'll put them on foot."

Luke interrupted, "If we can get them on foot, we can pick them off one by one on the road. It'll be to our advantage." Proudly, he added, "'Cause country boys know how to fight."

Katie frowned when Luke made reference to 'boys.' Unfortunately, he struck a raw nerve with this young independent from McAllister's Lane. Promptly, he tried to make amends. More humble now, he lowered his voice and said, "Of course, you too, Katie."

"Well, let's get busy," encouraged Mr. Cartwright. As soon as he spoke, doors and shutters were ripped from his house. Nails quickly hammered through from the underside would surely deter any pickup and put the members of the Klan on foot. The nailed boards were loaded onto Luke's vehicle. Everyone jumped on the back as Luke sped off down the road—that is, everyone except the beekeeper!

About a mile from their community, the group strategically laid the nailed boards across the narrow dirt road. They threw dirt on top to hide the wood, leaving the nails protruding from under the thin layer of soil. Luke backed his pickup into a side lane. Hiding behind trees, everyone quietly waited for the Klansmen to arrive.

A few minutes later, headlights from two trucks could be seen in the distance. According to Katie's last count, there were three vehicles. More than likely, one had been left at the barn with a blown-up motor. A faint chuckle emerged from her throat.

The lights approached nearer and nearer. Katie could feel her heart beating faster as anticipation increased. Within an instant, the first pickup crossed the boards. *Blam!* The front wheel tire blew, then the other front tire. Another *blam! blam!* All four tires blew out! Swiftly, the pickup following the lead one swerved to the right, barely missing the rear of the first vehicle. However, it plowed into a big oak. The front end crashed. A ruptured radiator sent hot steam billowing up. The Klansmen jumped out of the pickup, cursing and swearing as they realized their deplorable fate.

Katie's heartbeat quickened, as did her breathing, when the man from Texas stepped out of the vehicle. Immediately, he began shouting orders. "Two of you boys stay here and fix the flats! We're gonna need a fast way out of here as soon as we take care of our business with the preacher man." Waving his arms, he motioned the others to follow. "Let's go! We can walk the rest of the way. Preacher Smith's church is just down the road."

Strategically, Katie counted each and every man as they walked by. Two were not accounted for; that left eight. Her assumption was that the missing two had stayed at the barn to work on the other vehicle. More confident, she smiled. "The odds are looking better."

Luke motioned for Katie and the carpenter to stay behind to deal with the two Klansmen who remained to change the flat tires. Quietly, he eased along the edge of the woods behind the others steadily walking down the road to where Preacher Smith lived.

One of the men left behind reached for the jack in the back of the pickup. He explained to the other, "We'll take the tires off the wrecked truck and put them on the truck with the flats. I'll slide under and prop the jack under the axle. When I get it in place, you hand me the lever so I can jack it up."

Katie waited until the first man was completely underneath the vehicle. Slowly, she began easing out from behind the tree where she was hidden. While the man placed the jack under the axle, the other man knelt and waited to hand him the bar. Just as he knelt, a crashing blow to the head sent him sprawling to the ground. Grabbing the unconscious man by the legs, Katie pulled him into the woods.

The man under the pickup said, "Okay, Ben, hand me the bar." He extended his hand. Just as he grabbed it, someone holding the other end of the bar began to pull him out from under the pickup. "Whoa, Ben, what do you think you're doing?" he asked, trying to resist the pull of the tire tool.

As he was being dragged out from under the pickup, his eyes widened as he realized that it was *not* his friend Ben on the other end of the jack handle. It was Lester Cartwright, the carpenter from the black community. The man quickly released the bar and began scrambling and pushing himself backward under the pickup to the other side. Mr. Cartwright grabbed his legs by the ankles and pulled him out from under the truck.

The man screamed, "Ben! Where are you?"

Katie stepped from out of the darkness. "I'm sorry, but your buddy, Ben, can't come to your rescue at the moment."

Frightened, the man crouched. It was not often a pretty young woman stood before him with a Henry rifle aimed straight at his head. "Where is Ben?" he asked.

A slow, devilish smile crossed Katie's face. "Let's just say that he's tied up at the moment." The smile soon converted to a hard, tight mouth. "Now, get up. You're going to join him."

Willingly, the man, afraid of the woman with the Henry, obeyed. He was led to a big oak tree where Ben, obviously suffering from an enormous headache, was tied. Moaning, he asked, "What are you going do with us?"

Katie securely tied both men to the big oak. For a brief moment, she glared at both. "Well, that all depends on you, Ben. If you stay here like a nice little boy until I come back to get you, then I'll cut you loose. You and your buddy can walk back home." Suddenly, the tone of her voice became harsher and more intense. "But until then, if I should ever see your ugly face...." She poked him in the side with her rifle.

Mr. Cartwright interrupted Katie. "...she'll make sure that your tail hole favors your mouth hole so much that when you pass wind, you won't know which end to blow."

Ben gasped. His friend swallowed hard. Frightened out of their wits, both nodded their heads, confirming that they would do exactly as instructed.

Lester Cartwright said to Katie, "I know a shortcut. We can catch up with Luke."

Katie turned to go but abruptly turned back to the two men tied to the big oak tree. "Now, be sweet, fellas. Don't you go and do anything that's going to make me forget that I'm supposed to be mild-mannered and ladylike." A mischievous grin crept across her face as she darted into the darkness of the trees behind the carpenter.

And the Klansmen gasped!

Chapter 17

CONVENIENT TRAGEDY

Katie and the carpenter were crouching behind a tree. In the middle of the road a few yards ahead, the Klansmen walked steadily. Unaware of their stalkers, they stopped to receive last-minute instructions from the man with the silver slide.

"Now listen to me, men," he rumbled. "We'll search every house looking for the preacher. As soon as we find him, let's put a rope around his neck and drag him to the church." Sternly, the evil man searched their eyes to confirm they were listening. "We'll take him into the church and tie him to his pulpit." He paused. "Then we'll set fire to the church…and the preacher!"

His followers looked around at each other. By the expressions on their faces, this was more than they had bargained for, yet no one intervened. The man from Texas took out his white hood from inside his shirt and pulled it over his head. His followers did the same.

"Let's go! Let's show these heathens that white men have supremacy in this county!" he yelled before pressing on. Two abreast, they continued to trudge down the road.

At the edge of the woods, Katie reached for Mr. Cartwright and lightly touched him on the shoulder. She put her finger to her lips. "Shhh."

From inside her own shirt, Katie pulled out two Klansmen's hoods that she had taken from the pickup at Mr. Thoms's livestock facility. Mr. Cartwright pulled one over his head. Just as Katie started to do the same, a familiar, strong hand gently cupped her mouth. Instantly, she knew it was Luke. He shook his head, indicating a definite negative and took the hood out of Katie's hand.

He leaned closer to her ear and whispered, "Now it's my turn to have some fun." With a quick motion of his head, Mr. Cartwright, along with Luke, joined in at the back of the line the Klan had formed.

A few more yards down the road, one of the Klansmen dropped back. As he stooped to tie his shoe, Luke seized the opportunity. With the butt of his gun, he hit the man in the back of the head. The Klansman fell to his knees and then facedown in the dirt. Mr. Cartwright quickly dragged him to the side of the road and into the woods. From out of nowhere, two of the carpenter's young sons, watching from nearby, came out of the bush to aid their father. They carried a long staff and short piece of board.

One whispered to his father, "Can we help, Pa?"

Katie and the carpenter looked at each other and smiled. Proudly, the man handed his sons a piece of rope.

"Tie him up good and tight. When he comes to and tries to get away, give him a whop with your sticks."

The youngest son bared his big, shining teeth in a smile. The youngster asked his father, "Can we whop him good, Pa?"

Mr. Cartwright lovingly rubbed the top of the boy's head. "Yeah, son, you can whop him good."

Quickly, Katie and Mr. Cartwright pulled the hoods over their heads and scurried off to find Luke. Before they could catch up, the Klansmen had arrived at the black community where Preacher Smith lived. Katie anxiously scanned the hooded men. She knew that one of them had to be Luke, but which one?

The first house the Klan reached was the preacher's house. With the butts of their shotguns, several men broke down the door. Once inside the house, they overturned the furniture. They cast pots and pans to the floor. To their surprise, no one was inside.

One shouted out to the others, "No one is in here! Nary a soul!"

All the Klansmen ran inside Preacher Smith's house except for one. It was then that Katie realized that the man who chose to remain outside had to be Luke.

Quietly, she eased up behind him. Yes, it was Luke! The mere nearness of him made her heart flutter.

She whispered, "Having fun yet?"

Luke wheeled around. "Get out of here, Katie. Things are fixing to get ugly."

"I am not leaving, Luke," Katie replied. "Pretty soon, they're gonna be counting heads, and we've got to have enough bodies out here to make up for the men who are missing."

Luke kept watching the door for the Klansmen to come out. "I don't even want to know what you did with the others."

Katie snickered. Then, more seriously, she added, "We've got to come up with a plan, and soon. Have any ideas?"

"Not yet. Stay close just in case I do."

Confused, the men came charging out of the house. They did not understand where the preacher and his family were or why they had left the premises. No one was supposed to know about the raid except the few Klansmen who were at Mr. Thoms's barn.

The Texan ordered, "Split up. Half of you men look in the next house, and the other half, check out the others." Katie recognized the voice to be that of the leader. He growled, "Drag everybody out into the road. We'll beat the tar out of 'em until someone tells us where the preacher is hiding."

The next house belonged to the beekeeper, Mr. Odum. No one knew more about honeybees than Jeremiah Odum. For years, he had harvested the beehives and sold his precious honey in the nearby town. Perhaps he was the only man in ten counties who could walk among his bees and never get stung. His secret, he would often say, was, when walking among the bees, one should remain calm and not make any sudden movements. Swatting or running ensured the swarming, biting insects would attack. No one, for obvious reasons, could or would walk among the bees like Mr. Odum. No one tried! Mr. Odum also knew that the best time to move a beehive was at night. Dormant in their rest, the hive would willingly stay calm, unless it was greatly disturbed.

Katie and Luke assumed the reason Mr. Odum had not accompanied them earlier was that he had had a sudden change of heart. Little did they know that Mr. Odum's heart was indeed in the right place and that he would never forsake his neighbors. He fully intended to protect his home and his community. However, he had accessibility to a better means of assistance. With the help of his little stinging friends, anyone who attempted to invade his home would meet their own demise.

While the others were away placing the nailed boards across the road to blow truck tires, Mr. Odum had stayed behind. He bolted the only two windows in his house so that no one from inside could get out. Strategically, he placed a chair by the only door to his house—the front door. Then off he went to the hives to collect his precious bees.

Three Klansmen broke off from the others. When they stepped up onto Mr. Odum's porch, they noticed the door was ajar. Slowly and carefully, they entered. Immediately, Mr. Odum, who was hiding around the side of the house, sprinted around the corner and closed the door behind the trespassers. Quickly, he pulled the chair to fit snugly under the doorknob. The men, trapped inside, tried desperately to force open the door but failed.

Katie and Luke, slowly walking around to the rear of the house, saw Mr. Odum. They watched as he picked up a beehive and carefully climbed a ladder to the roof. Then he discreetly dropped the hive down into a hole he had made around the smokestack.

Luke glanced at Katie, smiling. He commented, "Now I'm having fun."

Almost immediately, horrific screams erupted from inside Mr. Odum's house. Frantic Klansmen yelled out as a mass of swarming, agitated bees clustered and repeatedly stung the trapped men. They pounded on the door and windows. Despite their efforts, they could not open either.

Mr. Odum spied Katie and Luke but did not recognize them with the hoods over their heads. Before they could inform him of their identity, he retreated into the nearby woods.

By now, the other Klansmen realized that someone had forewarned the community. The only living things found in the vacant homes were mangy dogs left lying tied under porches.

The man from Texas was furious. He gritted his teeth. Through the holes of his white Klan hood, squinted eyes could be seen. The Klansman barked, "Jasper, come with me to the church! We'll burn it down anyway. You other men check the last house, then come on down and see what I do to their church." Grumbling and snarling like a ravaging animal, he left.

The last house on the road belonged to Snake. At that time, the two Klansmen entering the house were unaware that something other than Snake lived in the small wooden shanty at the end of the road: his pets. Snakes! Long ones, big ones, small ones, but more dangerous than that, poisonous ones!

Shortly after the black families had fled to find safety within the woods, Snake took his uncanny slithering housemates out of their boxes and laid them on the floor of his house. Carefully, he placed his long staff behind a six-foot rattler's neck. Picking up the rattler, he quietly slipped out the door.

The two Klansmen slowly raised their guns as they tiptoed in through the front door. Cautiously, they eased through the house, which was dark inside—but not cautiously enough. All of a sudden, one man let out a bloodcurdling scream! He threw his gun down on the floor and grabbed his leg. As he was reaching for his leg, instantaneously, another fanged monster hissed and struck, hitting its target. Yelling, the Klansman limped outside on the porch, only to tumble and roll facedown in the dirt. His companion, realizing that he was surrounded by numerous eerie crawling and hissing reptiles, cried out for help. Soon, overcome by fright, he darted for the door, only to receive a bite from an inconspicuous rattler curled and waiting to strike.

Katie and Luke watched from outside. As soon as they realized that all but two men were incapacitated, they made a dash for the church. Inside, the man called Jasper was piling wooden benches around the pulpit where the preacher stood to deliver his sermons.

Luke turned to Katie. Pleading, he said, "I'm serious now, Katie. It's time for you to leave." At that moment, Mr. Cartwright scurried behind them. Luke continued, "Mr. Cartwright, you are going to have to stay outside, too. You can cover your face with that hood." Luke glanced down at the dark skin on Mr. Cartwright's hands. "But you can't cover up those."

Mr. Cartwright held up his hands. "Guess you're right, Luke." He smiled. "I'll go on back down the road where my boys are holding that man at bay. Bet by now, they've whopped him so many times, he's got knots all over his head." He chuckled as he turned to leave.

Luke turned back to Katie. He begged, "Please, Katie, go." Soft, serious eyes could be seen glaring from the two holes of the Klansman's hood. "I don't want anything to happen to you."

Although unwilling, Katie relented. Slowly, backing away, her gaze remained fixed on Luke. Ten steps backwards, then turning, she hurried away into the darkness.

Luke watched Katie disappear into the shadows of the night. Satisfied that she had gone to a place of safety, he turned towards the church. He sighed. "Dang it, my papa told me never to start a fight. But he also told me never to walk away from one."

Cautiously, Luke meandered his way to the front door of the church. Slowly, he raised his shotgun, ready for whatever doom was near.

"That's enough, boys," he calmly said. "Ain't gonna be no church-burning tonight."

Startled, Jasper and the Western man with the silver slide whirled around to see the intruder. Confused, they looked questioningly down the barrel of Luke McCoy's shotgun. Then, slowly, Luke removed the white pointed hood from his head. The Klansmen gasped.

The smell of kerosene poured on broken wooden pews sent a burning stench up Luke's nostrils. With shotgun held steady, he leisurely eased his way away from the door and over to the side of the two Klansmen.

"Move away from there," Luke ordered.

Hands held up, Jasper moved to the other side of the church. However, the man from Texas remained where he was standing. When he yanked the hood from his head, a lingering sneer was exposed.

"Sorry, son, but I came here tonight to burn a church down, and I intend to do just that."

The leader of the Klansmen lit a match and held it high. The reflection of the flames danced in the Westerner's evil eyes. The wicked man of destruction shifted a glance towards Jasper, then back to Luke.

"Besides, I don't think that you can kill both of us before one of us can get to you."

Before Luke had time to speak, a rifle fired from outside the door. The bullet zinged through the church, striking the tip of the match the Texan held in his hand. The flame from the match was extinguished!

The sound of an unexpected rifle shot startled the men, including Luke. All three jumped. Luke whirled to see who fired the rifle and from where. Just as Katie entered the door with rifle in hand, Jasper lunged. However, unknown to everyone, crouching above on the rafters of the church was Snake. Before Jasper could take more than a step, Snake released the six-foot rattler that he had been holding by the neck. Down fell the snake, twisting and turning, until it landed on top of Jasper's head. Jasper screeched, undoubtedly with fright, and then pain. Needless to say, the damage was done. The snake's sharp fangs struck deep into Jasper's neck, sending its deadly poison surging through his body.

The Texan snatched out his pistol and in the same instant pulled the trigger, sending a bullet through Snake's shoulder. Snake fell from the rafters and crashed onto the floor below.

In that moment, Luke turned to Katie and then to Snake. Luke had forgotten about the man with pistol. Before he could regain his senses, a hard blow to the head sent him sprawling on the hard wooden floor. The Texan had temporarily knocked him out with the butt of his gun. The Klansman turned to face Katie. Both held their breath. Less than ten feet separated the two adversaries. Katie's rifle, aimed between the dark, evil eyes of the man from Texas, was steady. And steady also was the Klansman's pistol aimed dead center at Katie's chest. The silence was eerie and yet frightening.

Finally, the Texan spoke, calmly and serenely. "I know who you are. You're Katie McAllister, the girl from McAllister's Lane."

"And you are the man from Texas."

He nodded. "So, we finally meet. I've heard folks from your neck of the woods talk about how Katie McAllister can hit a match on a fencepost at twenty paces." He chuckled, more with admiration than contempt. "Dang if you can't."

Rifle and pistol remained steady. Foes remained calculatingly calm.

"Why don't you put that rifle down and go on back home, Katie McAllister?" he said. "Why don't we just agree that this is a bad day for dying?"

"I don't plan to die, mister. But if I did, I wouldn't mind it a bit as long as I took a piece of you with me."

"So you want a piece of me?"

"I want all of you...six feet under."

Their stares were icy cold; their voices were composed yet serious.

"Why, Katie, are you threatening me?"

"You can call it a threat. But it's a statement, simple and true."

"So you *are* going to kill me?"

"If it's necessary."

"But why, my dear?"

"You are defiled and an abomination to all that is righteous."

"Now, Katie, Katie. You don't understand the entirety of the situation. Think about it for a second. I shoot you. You shoot me. It would be such a waste. And you would end up being just another convenient tragedy."

Suddenly, within that same moment, Snake made an attempt to move, and Luke groaned. Katie glanced to Luke and then to Snake. The man with the pistol made a lunge for Luke and jammed his pistol against Luke's temple.

Katie froze, uncertain what to do next. She wet her lips and took in a deep breath as her aim remained steady, straight at the Klansman's head. Now what?

"I'll make a deal with you, Katie," said the man, still holding the pistol at Luke's head. "Let me ease my way past you out that door. Let me take what's left of my men with me."

"Those that aren't dead, can't walk."

"They'll walk or they'll die trying. I never leave one of my men behind."

"How honorable of you," Katie joked.

"Don't get smart with me." The Klansman jammed the pistol tighter into Luke's temple. Luke moaned. Katie remained standing firm, still, and unrelenting.

"When I get down the road, I'll let your little farm boy go free."

"How will I know that you will do what you say?"

"Because I don't want to spend the rest of my life looking over my shoulder. That's how you can know that I will keep my word."

"Don't harm him!"

"Like I said, I don't want to spend the rest of my life looking over my shoulder."

While the man waited for a reply, the rattlesnake that Snake had thrown down from the rafters slithered its way between Katie's feet and out the door. The courageous woman from McAllister's Lane never even flinched. Steadfast, she remained focused; her aim remained fixed.

Luke stared at Katie. He was totally amazed at the guts and gall she calmly displayed. Never had he known a woman who could be soft and tender one minute yet in the next so calculatingly cold.

Again the Klansman spoke, appealing to her good sense. "All of us can die here tonight or none of us. What will it be?"

Katie could not bear it if she allowed anything to happen to Luke. With jaws tightly clenched, she slowly backed away from the door. Never once dropping her aim with her rifle, she helplessly watched as the Texan with the silver bolo slide walk out the door with a pistol shoved against Luke's temple. In less than a minute, he was gone.

Chapter 18

SANCTIFICATION

*D*awn approached, bringing forth a brilliant glow from a red morning sun, sending remnants of beams across patches of damp ground. A soft southerly breeze stirred. Mr. Cartwright rang the church bell loudly, signaling that it was safe for the families to return home. From out of their hidden retreat came Preacher Willy Smith along with his family and others. Small, frightened children held tenaciously to their mother's skirts. Infants cuddled at their mother's bosoms. The people from the small community gathered around the aging preacher. Anxiously, they waited for words of consolation and prayed for understanding.

Solemnly, Preacher Smith began, "My people, the good Lord has miraculously spared us."

An angry mother, with feelings of resentment and not understanding the persecution of her race, pulled her children close.

Preacher Smith noticed her disposition. He hastened to restore order and bring a sense of peace back to his frightened flock. "Listen to me, my children. The Negro race has a history of being rejected. We cultivate no outside friendships. We may be surrounded by a world that demoralizes us, but we must remain strong in this time of corruption. I pray for God to comfort you on this day, to give you confidence when you doubt and to increase your faith. I pray that He gives you courage and patience. Heed my words and repent of the anger in your heart. Cast it out. I beseech you. Remember the importance of family and having a God-centered life. Avert God's judgment upon you. God will take judgment upon those who are unrighteous."

"Amen," they replied in unison.

Preacher Smith's soothing words brought deliverance from their rage. A spirit of mutuality permeated the hearts of the forsaken people. They would rise from this ordeal and covenant to continue to serve God, their family, their church, and their community.

As Katie cleaned and dressed Snake's wound, she listened to the intense words of the wise preacher. Not once did he stop proclaiming God's word.

As for Katie, she wrestled with the ugliness of this nation's hate and prejudices. After all, the Lord had redeemed this race from slavery. She knew there was need for a greater redemption and revelation to stop this downward spiral of disobedience and injustice. In the midst of these condemnations, Katie prayed. She prayed for these people, for the nation, and for herself. She prayed that she would find her way back to the time when her faith was greater. She did not want to be in this place in her life feeling spiritually inept. The trauma that she had just endured left her bitter. How could she have allowed herself to go from a state of bitterness to forgiveness and now back to bitterness?

Katie closed her eyes, took a deep breath, and asked God to restore her trust and take away her feelings of wanting retribution. Longing for the time not so long ago when she was free from those feelings of hatred and resentment, she was overcome with the urge to return to the place where she once was, a place where she could once again learn to trust and forgive.

Some time ago, Katie's father had shared with her that forgiveness was not optional. Thomas McAllister emphasized that people could not be forgiven until they forgave those who trespassed against them.

Long past the time spent alone at McAllister's Lane, she became resolved to forgive those who had aligned themselves against the McAllisters and Kings. She made a promise to herself to do constructive deeds and show kindness to all people, especially those who trespassed her.

Mr. Cartwright, sensing her thoughts, spoke to her. "Have faith, Katie. Stop looking down at the dirt on your feet, child, and look up towards Heaven. There lies your answer."

Preacher Smith also genuinely expressed his feelings. As the two newfound friends walked to a quiet, solitary place, the preacher began, "Don't wonder about, ponder on, or obsess over what has happened here, Katie, in your life or in ours. Have faith that everything will work out for the best. God's grace and mercy will restore all of us."

"I don't think you quite understand, Preacher Smith. I was so close to killing the man who is responsible for my friend's death. I am so full of hate at this moment, and I don't know how to get back to the place where I was, a place where I had left bitterness behind me. There seems to be a bridge between where I am and the place where God wants me to be. It is like He is writing the story of my life, but I don't know where He is taking me."

"Sometimes, you must cross that bridge to allow God to carry out His plan for you. Sometimes, you must burn it down and build a new one. You say it is like God is writing your story. He has a plan for you, Katie. This is where trust and faith come into your story. You have to let Him show you the way. And more important, you have to *accept* His plan."

"I guess that's part of becoming sanctified," said Katie. "I mean, allowing God to make changes in your life so that you can grow in faith."

"Yes, and allow your trials and losses to help you grow. Faith is not a matter of hoping that God can make a change, but rather knowing that He will. You know, sometimes God will put a mountain in your way so that He can teach you that *faith* will change that mountain into a hill."

Katie felt sure that Preacher Smith did not understand the hurt and death that had contributed to her life's brokenness. She continued to make a desperate effort to explain.

"At first, after Son was killed, I was honestly a long way from believing that God had not deserted me. I was so bitterly angry. It was hard to let the past go and forgive those who had hurt me, Sadie, and our families. It was the worst trial that I have ever had to endure. I struggled to change. With the help of Papa, I thought that I had changed. But then, last night, I stood face to face with the devil. I wanted to take his life." Katie turned her eyes to those of the wise old preacher. "I feel like a ship sailing aimlessly, broken and beaten and without an anchor."

"There is a great boat maker and a great sail maker who can fix you and make you whole. Ask God to bring you peace and to be your anchor in the storm."

Out of her despair, Katie lifted her eyes and began to cry softly. "I don't know how, Preacher. I don't know how to pray and not to be bitter anymore. I feel nothing but numbness."

Preacher Smith began to reassure her. Soft and kind words resonated in Katie's soul. "There is a *stilling* in the heart, Katie. It is called *forgiveness*. In God's heart, forgiveness is never impossible. Be still, my child, and feel the power of the Lord doing His great work." He left Katie alone so she could contemplate and pray in solitude.

The breeze was gentle, silent, and serene. Warm rays of sunlight shined on her face as she looked up towards Heaven and cried out to God. Patiently, she waited for Him to send His mercy.

In that very moment, as she fervently prayed, she felt the stilling of the heart that Preacher Smith had referred to. In the beginning, she heard no voice and felt no presence. Indeed, she had never felt emptier. Then, suddenly, a prayer came unbidden to her lips.

"Lord, fill my emptiness with your presence. Stop the anger and fill my heart with forgiveness and Your presence. And, Father, please give me a sense of purpose and a sense of direction. Keep me in Your will and help me leave all the consequences to You."

As Katie silently prayed for God's presence, her heart was opened to reconciliation. It was as if a film were immediately lifted from her eyes. Not only was forgiveness made possible, but it filled the emptiness and stopped the anger. In a moment of grace, she felt the presence of the Holy Spirit. The stings and tendrils of hatred were broken as forgiveness set her free, just like a bird escaping from the hunter's snare. The shackles were broken and Katie was free. Once more, she weathered the storm as her soul found its anchor. God and sinner had reconciled.

After a while, Katie, now jubilant and self-assured, found the wise preacher. "I'm going to burn those bridges, Preacher Smith. I'm going to build another...a stronger one, one that will last. And no matter what His plan is for me, I will trust Him and have faith because His way is the best way."

"That's good. Move forward, my child. Little steps at first, then big steps, and never, never look back." Preacher Smith held Katie's hands in his. "Now, you go on and find that young man of yours, that McCoy boy. Let him lay the first plank on that new bridge."

"I will. I promise that I will find him. But what about you, Preacher Smith, and what about your people? What is going to stop this madness?"

"God is not going to desert us. He also has a mighty big plan for us. I believe that one day He'll send a great leader who will deliver us." A tear fell down his cheek. "One day we will have a leader who will lead us to freedom. Upon his back, the weight of segregation will be broken. The shackles will be torn apart. The dividing walls of hostility and prejudice that separate our people will come falling down. All men will be treated equally, with respect and with honor. For where God reigns, He will bring together into oneness those who by culture and by education are far apart." Preacher Smith's elegant words were spoken like a prayer, like the trusting supplication of an obedient child.

Discreetly, Mr. Cartwright interrupted. "Until that day, there is going to be a lot more heartache coming our way." He pointed to the community's beloved church that remained standing and unharmed. "And one day, years down the road, they'll come back, and they'll burn our church to the ground. The Klan always finishes what it starts."

Katie picked up her rifle and shook Preacher Smith's and Mr. Cartwright's hands. "Tell Snake to see a doctor as soon as he can with that arm. But now I have to go and find Luke." At that moment, a small child lovingly tugged at Katie's jeans and wrapped his small arms around her legs. Kneeling, Katie reciprocated the affection.

Suddenly, Mr. Cartwright yelled out, "Luke! There's Luke! He's coming down the road!"

Katie looked up from her embrace with the small child, and saw Luke moving slowly down the road towards her. Slowly she stood, brushing wet trails of tears from her cheeks. She quickly wiped them away before anyone could see. Then, unexpectedly, it did not matter if anyone knew how she felt about Luke. What was important was that he was safe and that he was walking to meet her.

Luke waved. Katie beamed and frantically waved back. Not able to contain her emotions any longer, she laid down her rifle and started walking towards him, slowly at first and then faster. Finally, she broke into a run—straight into Luke's outstretched arms. For a moment, they stood holding each other in a tender embrace. Preacher Smith and all of his community rushed forward, surrounding their heroes. Under the infinite sky, the sound of the people of the small black community singing and clapping their hands filled the air. An unspeakable joy and a newfound love encased Luke and Katie as they embraced.

Later, Luke and Katie said their good-byes. Sadly, they began their drive back to Mr. Thoms's barn. Further down the road, Luke reached for Katie's hand and held it tightly in his.

"What are we gonna do now?"

"For now, we go to our homes. I have to go back to McAllister's Lane."

Luke pulled a chain out from under his shirt. On the end was a ring made of braided horsetail. "This is the hair from the tail of a horse of mine." He pulled the chain over his head and handed it to Katie. "My mama made this necklace and put it around my neck. When I left home, she told me that she wanted me to carry something with me that would remind me of my roots." He paused. "So I would always remember the place and the people I love."

Katie took the necklace from Luke's hand. Her fingers rubbed the coarse, braided hair from the horse this man greatly loved. She lifted her eyes to meet his.

Luke parked the pickup near the side of the road. He took the necklace from Katie's hand and gently put it around her neck. He spoke soft words to his beloved. "This is to remind you that there is someone who will always love you." Then he chuckled. "My pa always told me that if I ever found a woman who was as pretty as a speckled puppy, as sweet as puddin' pie, and hard as nails, that I should ask her to marry me."

Although overjoyed, Katie's heart was breaking. She knew she never wanted to leave this jovial country boy with the dark eyes who had a way of making her melt with the mere nearness of him. However, she also knew she had to go home, back to McAllister's Lane.

Luke raised Katie's hands to his lips and tenderly kissed her fingers. His words painted the picture. "I watched a rattlesnake slide between your feet and out through a door. You never even blinked your eyes. And later, I saw you kneel down and put your arms around a small, frightened child to comfort him." He kissed her hands again. "Woman, you simply amaze me."

The drive back to Albany was silent. In the midst of the silence, there was sadness. In an effort to cling to the tenderness she felt from Luke's presence, Katie slid over on the seat near him. Their bodies were close, seeming to melt into each other, as did their eyes.

When they arrived at Mr. Thoms's livestock barn, Luke stopped at Katie's pickup. Katie got out and walked over to the window on his side of the truck. No further words needed to be said. Their expressions said it all. Luke smiled, shifted into first gear, and drove away back to his home.

Katie would soon leave in the opposite direction for her home—McAllister's Lane. She kept her eyes fixed on Luke's vehicle as it sped away. Slowly, her fingers found the necklace that Luke had placed around her neck. The braided horsetail ring found its way to her lips. Reminiscing on their short time together caused her to smile.

"And he never even kissed me."

Chapter 19

LOVE RETURNS

*H*ands held tight in union during a moment of prayer bound together the Kings and McAllisters as they sat down to eat their meager Sunday noon meal. With bowed heads, Sadie, Jezra, and Katie reverently listened as Thomas McAllister paused to give thanks for the food of which they were about to partake.

Humbly, he began, "Lord, bless this food that this family is about to take as its nourishment. For we…"

A loud knock at the kitchen door silenced Thomas. Everyone looked up to see who the visitor might be. An unkempt man in his mid-thirties with a prominent set of whiskers stood looking through the door.

Thomas called out to the man, "Come on in, stranger. We're fixin' to eat some dinner and more than willing to share what little we have."

The stranger, hesitant at first, and then entered. "Is this place called McAllister's Lane, and are you folks the McAllisters?"

"I reckon that's right," answered Thomas.

"My name is Eli Walton. I'm from over near the Georgia–Bamie line." He rubbed his rough, unshaven chin. "Met some folks on the rail turnabout. Think they were headin' to Birmingham."

Katie perked up, anxious to hear any news concerning her friends. "The Hamptons?" she inquired.

"Yep. Think that be their name. Anyways, I told them I was headed this way. They said to look you up if I wanted a mighty fine meal."

Thomas looked at the plate of fried ham, biscuits, and mustard greens. "We don't have much. But like I said, we are willing to share."

Eli nodded his head. "Yes sir, that looks like mighty fine eatin' to me." Then, staunchly, he glanced at Sadie and Jezra. His eyes narrowed with contempt. Silence momentarily filled the room, indicative of the boorish man's disapproval. Callously, he sat quietly and waited for the black couple to leave.

Katie sensed tension emerging within the room. However, she asked, "Aren't you going to sit down, Mr. Walton?"

Eli shifted his weight and scuffed his feet. "Ma'am, I don't sit down at no table with folks of color."

Sadie moved to rise from the table. Almost instantaneously, Katie grabbed her arm and pulled her back down to her chair.

Thomas intervened. "Let me explain something to you, Mr. Walton. We are a God-fearing people. In this house, we obey all of God's commandments, and the most important is to love one another. As a family, we show love in many ways. One is by accepting others for who they are."

Eli frowned. He still showed contempt.

Thomas went on to say, "I guess that I need to set the plow a little deeper so that you can understand. These folks are not going to leave on account of you. So unless you are willing to sit at this table, then, sir, I guess you are going hungry today."

Eli glanced at Jezra, then back at Thomas. Realizing that he was outnumbered, he had to comply if he wanted to eat. Long, rugged days riding the rails with an empty, aching stomach was reason enough for Eli to seriously contemplate the situation. Finally he relented, removed his dirty hat, and pulled out a chair.

Even after the obnoxious man's insult, Sadie displayed kindness. "I'll get you a plate, Mr. Eli."

Resignedly, Eli nodded, showing his appreciation.

The rest of the meal was eaten in silence. Eli gobbled his food, shoveling it into his gullet. As he slurped and lapped the mustard juice, his atrocious manners disgusted Katie, forcing her to turn her head and look in another direction.

After they finished eating, the men walked out on the porch while Katie and Sadie cleared the table.

Sadie leaned over and whispered to Katie, "I don't think I like that man."

"I don't think that I like him, either. Soon as he rests a bit, we'll send him on his way."

"Did you see the way he was looking at you?" asked Sadie.

"Not really. I couldn't stand watching him eat. I've seen dogs with better manners."

Sadie giggled. She looked around to see if anyone was listening; then she lowered her voice. "He was looking as if he wanted to get at you like he was gettin' at that food."

Katie sighed as she looked over her shoulder at the despicable man sitting on the porch next to Thomas. "He'll be gone soon."

When they had finished cleaning the kitchen, Katie and Sadie sat down at the table to talk. Hands folded, Sadie leaned forward.

"Now, tell me more 'bout this handsome young man you met at Mr. Thoms's livestock barn. Tell me again how every time you looked at him, your heart beat so fast that it made you plum dizzy."

Sadie's frivolousness made Katie laugh. "I didn't say that I got dizzy. I just said that my heart beat fast."

Sadie gently patted Katie's hand. "Child, it hasn't been that long ago since ol' Jezra made my heart beat fast. And that made me dizzy!"

As Katie remembered the promises of the young man with the coal black eyes and hair, her fingers found their way to her neck. She squeezed the horsehair braided ring that Luke had placed around her neck. Almost six weeks ago, she had parted ways with Luke at the livery barn in Albany. Since that day, she had not heard from or seen him. Her eyes burned as she swallowed hard, trying to hold back tears. She thought that sincerity, not hypocrisy, was characteristic of Luke McCoy. At the moment, she was wondering if she had misjudged the young man.

"I don't guess it matters how he made me feel," Katie said through teary eyes. "Undoubtedly, he didn't feel the same way." She jerked her hand away from the necklace, then quickly wiped away a fallen tear that had slowly crept down her cheek. "He's forgotten about me already."

Sarah said, "Yep, it's *love* all right!"

"Love?"

"Yes ma'am. When the memory of your man sneaks out of your eyes and rolls down your cheeks, it's definitely love."

"How do you love someone, Sadie, when you can't trust? I trusted that I would see him again, and now he has let me down. Listen, Sadie, I may have thought once that I could trust Luke, but I for sure won't be stupid enough to do it again!"

Forgotten promises caused Katie's tender heart to break. She sniffed at the thought that she possibly could have misjudged the jovial country boy.

Sadie grinned. "Yep. Definitely *love!*"

At that moment, Thomas walked through the door. "Told Eli that he could stay on a couple of days."

Sadie's and Katie's eyebrows crinkled; their mouths tightened.

Thomas continued, "Told him I'd let him do some chores around the place for his meals. The fields need tending, and we can use the help."

Disgusted and disappointed, the two frustrated women did not reply. Most definitely, Thomas's decision was not of their choosing. Katie shoved her chair back and stormed out of the room.

Confused, Thomas watched as his daughter angrily stomped through the doorway. "Did I do something wrong, Sadie?"

Sadie stood. Wringing the dish towel she held in her hands, she barked, "You men! Sometimes I don't know who is the dumbest, a dang ol' mule or a dang ol' man. I do wonder what ya'll use between your ears, 'cause it sho' ain't brains."

Thomas's brow furrowed when it became evident that he had upset Sadie. Generally, she never used this tone of voice with him, especially with such harsh and contemptible words. However, more importantly, he realized that he had upset Katie. He decided to find his daughter and apologize.

As Thomas began to walk towards the door, Sadie yelled, "Don't go after her, Mr. Thomas! Let her be to herself for a bit."

Thomas didn't understand, but a quick nod implied that he did.

Sadie added, "And in the meantime, you best keep a close eye on that fella on the porch! I wouldn't trust him in an outhouse with a muzzle!" She walked over to the door and glared out at the man called Eli. With raised eyebrows and arms firmly folded across her chest, she whispered, "Better watch that one real good."

That afternoon, Jezra, Eli, and Katie meandered to the field to hoe weeds. Down the long rows of planted sweet potato, Katie observed the vines burgeoning with lush, green growth. Underneath in the rich, warm soil were the fruits of their labor and their hopes for their future. Sweet potatoes! Who would have ever guessed that in a land where cotton had always been the 'king' crop, sweet potatoes would grow? The king's reign was over. The majesty of the South of verdant bush and white-topped down was no longer sovereign, its superfluous crown discarded by a second harvest.

In the field, the blistering sun beamed hot on Katie's head. After several hard hours of work, hands tender from the grip on the hoe handle were dirty and sore. Finally, in the near distance, the distinct sound of the supper bell could be heard.

"That's Sadie callin' us to come in to eat," said Jezra excitedly. Hunger pains gnawing in his stomach indicated it had been a while since he had eaten.

At the well, Jezra drew a bucket of water and poured the cool, refreshing liquid over his head. As Eli washed his hands and face, he noticed Katie slipping away to the barn for privacy. Well hidden behind a stall, she dampened her bandana and washed the dirt from her body. Slowly, she unbuttoned her blouse. Tilting her head backwards, she squeezed the drenched bandana, allowing the cool water to flow down her neck to refresh her stinging skin.

Unaware that an intruder had invaded her privacy, she began to button her blouse as she turned to leave.

A seductive smile crossed the impious face of Eli Walton. His lurid eyes ravished Katie's body. "Don't stop. I'm enjoying watching you. And I like what I see."

Eli's presence startled Katie. "What are you doing in here, Eli? You know this is my private time. You're supposed to be with Jezra." She attempted to shove her way past him, but the undignified man blocked her exit. Angry, she blurted out, "Let me by or else!"

Once more, Katie attempted to push Eli to the side yet failed. Forcibly, he thrust her against the side of the stall. With one hand, he groped her body, and with the other, he held her mouth. Shoved backward, she fell onto the ground.

Eli pressed his body against hers as he tried to kiss to her mouth. He mumbled, "You're goin' to do what or else?"

With all of her strength, Katie kicked and fought back, but Eli was the stronger. She thought she was doomed to suffer Eli's abuse until a firm, strong hand grabbed him by the collar. Yanked backwards by an unknown hand, Eli landed on the ground.

A voice that Katie soon recognized calmly spoke. "Or else I'm gonna kick your nasty tail all the way down that road and back." It was Luke!

Quickly, Katie scrambled to her feet. Eli sprawled backwards when Luke's fists sent a crashing blow to his jaw. Slowly, he got up and raised his hands to say 'enough', picked up his hat, brushed his clothes off, and walked out the door.

For a while, Luke watched as Eli walked down the lane, away and out of their lives. Luke shook his hand and kissed his stinging knuckles. Then he chuckled, "Dang it, Katie! Do all the hired help have jaws made of steel? 'Cause if they do, then I'm just gonna let the next one have his way with ya."

Katie was not sure if she should be angry at Luke's fun-loving remark or angry because she had not seen or heard from him in weeks. In heated confusion, she brushed past Luke and stormed across the floor of the barn.

Luke scurried to catch the infuriated young woman. Just before she reached the big barn doors, he grabbed Katie by the shoulders and whirled her around. She lifted her eyes to meet his. Luke gently brushed Katie's hair from her forehead.

"Do you honestly think that I could ever allow any man to touch you other than me?"

Stunned, Katie remained silent. Just the thought of Luke's touch made her want to collapse in his arms. "I thought that you had forgotten me."

Luke pulled Katie into his arms. His lips brushed against her soft cheeks, inhaling her sweet fragrance. "You silly girl. How could I ever forget you?" Gently, he tilted her chin so that her blue eyes would meet his dark ones. He smiled, sure that he was winning this confrontation. "Not in a million years could I ever forget you." Playfully, he touched the tip of her nose. "That's because I am in love with you, Katie girl. And I have come to ask you to marry me."

Their lips became immersed in a tender embrace. As they savored the sweetness of each kiss, they cleaved tightly together, melting into each other's arms. John Luke McCoy had come to McAllister's Lane to substantiate his claim upon Katie's hand in matrimony. As for Katie, she was absolutely sure that she was willing.

Within that same moment, Sadie said to Thomas McAllister, "I think I'll walk out to the barn and see what's keeping Katie." Just as she opened the back door and stepped out onto the porch, Sadie looked up and saw Katie embracing a striking young man. Instantly, she knew that he had to be Luke McCoy. She smiled as she watched them become engrossed in each other's arms. Quietly, she stepped back into the kitchen before being noticed.

Thomas asked, "What's wrong, Sadie? You're smiling like a goat eatin' briars. Is Katie all right?"

"Oh, yes sir, Mr. Thomas. Katie is just fine." Sadie's face beamed, overcome with joy. "Yep. All is right with our Kat, and everything is going to be just fine."

And the barn sparrows chirped.

Chapter 20

A PROMISE TO LOVE

For what seemed like hours, Katie and Luke strolled through the beautiful South Georgia woods. Down beaten paths and across running brooks, Luke followed Katie as she shared with him every inch of the precious McAllister land that she so dearly loved. It was if Katie was experiencing for the first time the scents, the sounds, and the beauty of her home.

Together they watched as a lone soaring eagle sailed on the wind currents above. They caught sight of a scampering gray squirrel. A pair of turtledoves and meadowlarks made their presence known by their familiar songs. The audible songs of the birds echoed the song in their hearts.

However, no matter what Katie showed Luke of this wondrous land, his eyes always came back to meet hers. Captivated by her charm and beauty, there was nothing she could share that could surpass what he saw when he gazed into her eyes. Once Luke heard a wise woman say, "You can't make someone love you. All you can do is be someone who can be loved, and the rest is up to the person to realize your worth." More and more, he realized Katie's worth and prayed that she valued his. For now and ever, he knew that he loved this woman from the depths of his soul, with every breath he took, and with every beat of his heart.

On the porch, Thomas paced. Finally exhausted, he reclined in his rocker. "Where do you think they are? Why aren't they here by now?" Impatiently, he wrung his hands as he waited for their return. "You know, I think it was mighty rude of Katie to just take that young man off gallivantin' before we even had a chance to meet him."

Sadie, overflowing with joy as well as anticipation, chuckled. "Now, settle down, Mr. Thomas. From everything Katie told me about this young man, I know that she is in good hands." Despite her belief that no harm was coming to Katie, she, too, strained her eyes to catch a glimpse of the two. "They need a little time to themselves. And besides, Katie wants to show her young fella around."

"Did Katie say that this McCoy boy lived on a farm, too? Why does she think that this place is so different from his? Seems to me that dirt looks like dirt no matter where you live," Thomas scoffed.

"There's a lot about Katie that you don't understand, Mr. Thomas," Sadie replied. "Besides, this little piece of land is special to her, and she wants to show this place to her Luke."

In a comforting tone, she added, "Now, settle down. They be back soon."

Thomas continued rocking hard, almost setting the chair on the tips. "Well, how do they know they can get along? I mean, they haven't known each other long enough. Just how do they know?"

Sadie stifled a giggle as she noticed Thomas's chair was on the verge of coming off the rocker. "Long-tailed cats and porch rockers don't get along, Mr. Thomas, and if you don't calm down, that rocker is gonna set you on the floor!"

Within that same moment, Thomas glanced up and saw Katie and Luke walking towards them down the lane. Anxiously, he yelped, "Here they come, Sadie!" He stammered. "What, what do I do? What, what do I say?"

"Shhh, be quiet!" Sadie picked up a piece of oak wood. Handing it to Thomas, she ordered, "Here, whittle on this. Keep your hands busy, and keep your mouth shut. If you don't open your mouth, you can't stick your foot in it. Don't you dare say one word to embarrass that child."

"But what if he asks me a question?"

"Well, if you can't think of nothing to say, then tell him to ask me."

Quickly, Sadie sat down in the rocker next to Thomas, straightened her dress, and began humming a song. Thomas nervously reached inside his pocket and withdrew his pocketknife. Whistling the same tune as Sadie hummed, he began to nonchalantly whittle on the piece of wood.

Katie and Luke walked up onto the steps of the porch. Luke extended his hand. "Howdy, Mr. McAllister."

Thomas leaned forward and shook Luke McCoy's firm hand. "Howdy."

Luke said, "My name is Luke McCoy."

"Yeah, I know."

Sadie cleared her throat.

Thomas cast a knowing glance towards Sadie. Her eyes narrowed as an exasperated eyebrow was raised at the anxious father.

Thomas humbled himself, almost sinking into his seat. "Please to meet ya."

Luke turned to Sadie, tipping his hat. "Howdy, ma'am. You must be Sadie?"

Sadie beamed. Instantly, she liked this young man named Luke, who seemed to be well trained in the art of good manners, especially when it came to ladies of another race.

Luke showed no reluctance. "Well, Mr. McAllister, I'm gonna come straight to the point." He took a deep breath. "I'm here to ask you for your daughter's hand in marriage. "

Caught off guard, Thomas gasped. "Well, boy, you sure don't beat around the bush, do you?"

Once again, Sadie cleared her throat and glared at Thomas, signaling him to watch his manners.

This time, Thomas leaned forward and cocked an eyebrow towards Sadie, reciprocating her well-defined body language. He was almost on the verge of speaking but thought it best to refrain for the moment, careful not to misalign himself with the woman setting next to him on the porch. Steadily, he went back to whittling on the piece of oak, attempting to remain focused on the wood he held in his hand. Finally, he spoke. "Guess you'd better ask Sadie."

Sadie covered her mouth, attempting to suppress a giggle, but failed. Instead, overcome with joyful bliss, she burst into a laugh. "By gosh, you sure don't waste any time in saying what you want." She dabbed wet eyes with the hem of her apron. "I know that she loves you." She leaned forward and looked directly at Luke. "But do you love her?"

"With all my heart," Luke answered with confidence.

Sadie began to rock as she crowed, "Well, that ain't good enough!"

Katie gasped but remained silent, not sure what Sadie's intentions were for being so blunt. She also realized the importance of not being defiant when it came to Sadie. After all, she trusted Sadie's intuitive ability more than anyone she knew.

Just as startled was Luke. "But Miss Sadie, that's loving her a lot."

"Not in my book," confronted Sadie. "For me to say that you can have my Katie in marriage, you got to love her with more than just your heart. You got to love her to the heavens and back and with all your soul. You got to say you love her every night and prove it every day. Otherwise, a marriage can't take root."

"Oh," was Luke's only response.

Katie glanced at Luke, as did Thomas, and she waited for Luke to reply.

Sadie was straightforward. "Let me tell you something about being in love, son. In a blink of an eye, everything can change. So you have to love with all you have in ya. You may never know when it's taken away. "

After a brief interval, Luke spoke, using carefully well thought-out words so as to allay Sadie's concerns. It was important to procure her support. "Well, Miss Sadie, then I guess I have your blessing 'cause I love this woman with every bit of me. I love her with my heart, my soul, and anything else that I may have inside of me...and a little bit else on the side. I'll tell her every night and prove it every day. And of course, I promise to love her to the heavens and back." In contrast to his normally gregarious character, he shyly bowed his head. "And further than that, if I need to. "

Katie expelled a sigh of relief as Sadie smiled, showing her approval.

Knowing the importance of being honest and sincere in words and actions, especially in the matters concerning Sadie's concern for Katie, Luke added, "And if you will let me have her for my wife, I promise that I'll always, always take care of her and guard her with my life."

Luke's promises brought consolation to both Sadie and Thomas. It was clear that his pledge would be everlasting because it was unconditionally written upon his heart.

Thomas spoke. "And never lay a hand to her?"

Luke complied. "No sir. Not ever."

Sadie's and Thomas's eyes met. Simultaneously, they nodded, showing their approval. Sadie gleamed as jubilation welled inside. "Well, all is right with me. How 'bout you, Mr. Thomas?"

"I reckon so. I mean, I guess if *you* think so, Sadie."

Luke reached for Katie. He clasped her hand in his and gently squeezed, thankful beyond measure that this confrontation with Sadie was over.

At that moment, Thomas's pocketknife slipped and nicked his finger. Blood trickled.

Sadie quickly jumped to her feet and shielded the newly betrothed couple's view from the blood oozing from Thomas's finger. "Don't look!" she yelled. "Don't you dare look at that blood!"

Astonished as well as confused, Katie and Luke looked questioningly at Sadie.

"An ol' wives' tale among my people says that the first thing a couple sees right after the proposing will surely be the mark of things to come." Sadie looked behind her and motioned Thomas to hide his bloody finger. "That's why you mustn't look at the blood."

Katie had heard most of Sadie's old wives' tales, but never this one. On the other hand, Luke had no inkling of what Sadie meant. Nonetheless, the couple turned their heads, if for no other reason than to humor Sadie.

Luke spent the rest of the day and part of the next with his beloved Katie. In the afternoon of the next day, Katie drove him to the train depot in a neighboring town. Farewells were hard, but were soon reconciled with promises of never-ending love and a short engagement.

"As soon as the harvest is in, I'll return for you, Katie," promised Luke. "This will be the last time that we will ever have to be apart. I'm taking you back home with me as my wife. My home will be your home forever till the end of time."

Luke held Katie tightly in his arms as he kissed away fallen tears. He tasted their salt. Softly, he whispered in her ear, "When one of us cries, the other will taste salt."

Katie looked up at him through blurred eyes. "Where are your tears?" she asked.

"In my heart."

Katie buried her face in Luke's shoulder. She could feel his shirt become wet with her silent, heart-wrenching tears. "Sadie says that I would know when I had found the one who would love me back."

"How is that?" asked Luke.

"A man who truly loves you allows his shoulder to be wet with your tears. A man who does not love you has no idea that you are even crying."

"Your Sadie is a wise lady. "Luke smiled. "And guess what, Katie? I don't have one shoulder. I have two."

The westbound train came to a screeching halt. Passengers unloaded at the depot as others boarded to travel further west. Getting off the train were a few men of doom. Satan's emissaries had arrived! Ten men, gruff and boisterous in disposition, stepped off the train. Mysterious eyes scanned the streets of this peaceful little town. Picking up their baggage, they slowly started walking in the direction of the hotel. Suddenly, one of the men, recognizing Katie and Luke, stopped in his tracks. Enthralled by their sad farewells, the two never even noticed the terrifying man of evil.

The train whistle blew. The big engine puffed and sent billowing smoke and steam out from under its belly. Slowly, it began to chug along.

"All aboard!" the impatient conductor hollered once more to Luke, who was reluctant to leave.

One last embrace, and then Luke hopped on the side step. He waved as Katie frantically waved back. Then Luke stepped inside the passenger car as the train rolled on down the tracks.

Katie stood and watched as the passenger train disappeared on the horizon. She threw one last kiss to the much-loved man she had promised herself to in marriage. The stranger stealthily approached from behind her. Never suspecting that he was behind her, she turned to go. Face to face they stood; their gazes locked. Katie froze as she stared into the steel-cold eyes of the man from Texas, the man who wore string tie around his neck with a silver slide!

Quickly, Katie tried to evade the deplorable man. She attempted to push her way around him but miserably failed. The stranger grabbed her arm so tightly, she could not move.

"Let go of me!" she demanded.

Cold and harsh was his laugh. "Look here, boys," he bragged to his traveling companions, who had now gathered around. "If it ain't Katie McAllister from McAllister's Lane." He continued to jeer and gawk at the woman he greatly desired. His hands pressed deeper into Katie's arms.

Katie squirmed. "You're hurting me!" She turned to take one last look at the distant train, praying that by some miracle Luke had seen the Klansman.

The man from Texas forced Katie to look at him. He laughed despicably as he said, "Your farm boy is gone. He ain't coming back."

Once more, Katie unsuccessfully struggled to free herself. "I said to let me go!" she ordered.

This time, the harasser pulled Katie's face close to his. "I'm gonna let you go, all right. You run on back to McAllister's Lane and tell those black folks that I'm coming." He buried his nose in Katie's hair. "Tell them that I'm coming to finish the job that I started."

The annoying man pulled Katie's lips to his, pressing hard on her mouth. There was a brief struggle. Then she bit his lip hard. Blood spurted. He thrust Katie backwards, almost knocking her down. He yanked his handkerchief out of his rear pocket and pressed it against his lip to stop the bleeding.

It was then that Katie saw her chance to get free. She dashed to her pickup, never looking back. From nearby, she heard the Texan yell, "Tell 'em I'm coming, Katie! Tell 'em they can't hide 'cause I'll burn everything in sight till I find them."

What Katie did not hear were his whispered words spoken sultrily under his breath. "And I'm coming for you, Kathryn McAllister. I'm coming for you. And you are going to be mine."

Chapter 21

FIERY INDIGNATION

Backs bowed, Thomas McAllister and Jezra King hoed the grass around the sweet potato vines. Suddenly, in the near distance, they heard the sound of a honking horn. Inquisitive, keen eyes stared down McAllister's Lane. The old, rusty pickup came barreling towards them down the dirt road. Clouds of dust hovering in midair obscured their view. At the washpot, Sadie dropped her clothes. As she ran to the yard's edge, she cupped her hands over her eyes to see who was causing all of the commotion. The truck screeched to a halt.

Katie bounded out, frantically yelling, "Papa, Jezra, come quick!"

Thomas threw his hoe down on the ground. "Let's go, Jezra! Something is wrong! Katie was driving down that lane like a bat out of Hades."

Hurriedly, Thomas ran to Katie. Out of breath, he inquired, "What's wrong, Kat? You're scaring the wits out of us!"

The expression on Katie's face showed the seriousness of the message she was to deliver. Battling for words, she gasped, "Papa, the Klansmen are in town! They're coming here tonight! They're going to raid McAllister's Lane and burn everything to the ground!" Katie hurried to her beloved Sadie and started pushing her towards the house. "You and Jezra have got to leave! They're going to kill you! You've got to run and hide."

Wide-eyed and frightened, Sadie tightly clasped her apron. "But why are they coming out here to do us harm? Ain't killing my boy enough?"

Frantically, Katie continued to push Sadie towards the house. Almost within the same moment, she whirled to face her dearly loved friend. Holding her at arm's length, Katie exclaimed, "They want to destroy us, Sadie! They want to destroy us because we represent to them a way to love that they don't understand."

Sadie cocked her head sideways, grasping for understanding from Katie's words. "But why?"

"It's the Klan, Sadie. They do not want whites and blacks to love and care and respect each other...the way we do. We love with the heart, not the skin." Beseeching eyes burned with stinging tears as she continued to explain, "They want the whites to remain superior. They think that by destroying us, they destroy what we represent to this community: a fair, loving, accepting family who accepts their fellow man for whatever color they happen to be."

Engulfed with sorrow and despair, Sadie wilted. What was the inadvertent sin that would cost her life on the basis of her race? Her voice, hurting and strained, struggled with words. "I never meant any harm. All I ever wanted was to be near you, Katie, and to love you."

Katie pulled Sadie into her arms, cleaving to her as tears tore at her fragile heart. Tenderly, Katie embraced the woman who was the only mother she had ever known. "And that's all I ever wanted, Sadie." Katie cupped Sadie's sorrowful face in her hands. "You have done no wrong. Do you hear me? It's just that we are living in perilous and violent times. It's just that people today have to have someone to blame all their troubles on. So they blame those people who are different. This is not your fault. Understand?"

Sadie lowered her eyes, attempting to avoid Katie's. Katie lifted Sadie's chin, forcing the older woman to look into her eyes. Softly, she explained, "There is nothing wrong with loving people. It doesn't matter what color they are. All hearts look the same. Underneath a person's skin, all of us bleed the same color of blood."

Katie brushed the tears that were streaming down Sadie's face. More sternly now, she said, "Now, listen to me. You and Jezra go in the house and get enough provisions to last you for a couple of days."

Katie looked directly at Jezra. "Take her deep into the woods and hide." Her tone became harsher as she added, "No matter what happens, don't come out of hiding until this is over."

Sadie turned to go. Once again, Katie pulled her dearest friend into her arms. "Never forget how special you are to me. You are not insignificant. You are special, and you have more good in you than anyone I know. Always remember that the most important part of who you are is what's inside of you."

A wave of dizziness washed over Katie, causing her to feel flushed. Her knees trembled as her voice softened. "If something happens to me tonight, don't worry about me. We'll meet again. In Heaven. With Son." She chuckled, trying to lighten the situation. "You can rock me again like you did when Son and I were babies."

Sadie forced a smile and then hurried into the house to gather food and blankets. When she was inside, Jezra said, "When I get Sadie hid, I'll come back to help."

"No!" Katie ordered. Then, in a much quieter voice, she explained. "It doesn't matter if you are here to help us. We'll still be outnumbered." She looked at Thomas for support. "If we let them come in here and burn us out, then maybe they'll spare my and Papa's lives as long as we don't put up a fight." She looked back to Jezra. "But if you and Sadie are here, there'll be a killing for sure."

Jezra concurred, realizing that leaving was the only way to survive this horrific act of deadly vengeance inflicted upon them by the Klan. If he stayed behind, destruction was assured. Death was imminent.

Sadie ran out of the house with a bundle in her arms. Katie gave her a reassuring smile that all would be okay. At least, she hoped so.

Just as Jezra turned to follow Sadie into the woods, Katie grabbed his arm. "Wait a minute, Jezra." She reached for the braided necklace that Luke had placed around her neck. For a brief moment, she held it close to her bosom. Then, handing it to Jezra, she choked back tears. "If anything should happen..."

"Yes, Katie."

"Please give..."

Jezra took the necklace from Katie's trembling hand. "I understand. I'll give it to Luke."

Although Katie tried to remain composed, she knew that there was no need to minimize the tragedy that was upon them. Lamentation and horror would soon be visiting her beloved McAllister's Lane.

Holding fast but wavering, she boldly commanded Jezra. "Go! Go deep in the woods!" Katie stood and watched her much-loved Sadie and Jezra scurry off to hide in the confines of the trees. She whispered, "Take care, Sadie. And please, don't ever look back."

Later, an eerie stillness engulfed this place called McAllister's Lane. Darkness and gloom hovered. It was as if this gracious little home nestled in the backwoods of South Georgia knew that her days of being the cornerstone of the McAllisters for generations would soon be ending.

A gentle breeze stirred to cool the night. The crisp air blowing across Katie's face served as a solemn reminder that although life on this treasured piece of earth still existed, there was the possibility that the end of an era was near at hand. Katie shivered as she solemnly sat on the porch next to her father, awaiting unwelcome guests and the inevitable coming destruction. Their eyes, straining to see through the darkness, burned as they waited fearfully and with uncertainty.

Finally, in the midst of their apprehension and sorrow, Thomas broke the silence with a tender affirmation. "Katie, I love you."

"I love you, too, Papa," was her reply.

"No matter what happens to us tonight…" Thomas could not finish his statement. He cleared his throat, collected his thoughts, and started again. "Our life is in the hands of our Almighty God. Great is His faithfulness."

Katie smiled. "He promised that He would never leave us or forsake us. Tonight, I'm holding Him to it."

"He also said, 'Fear not,' but I sure am having a hard time with that one!" said Thomas.

Suddenly, a glimmer of light appeared down the lane. Loudness overpowered the quietness of the night. Pickups and men on horseback raced towards the McAllisters' home. It was soon evident that the glittering lights were torches.

Horrified by the sight, Katie tightly gripped the arms of the rocking chair. Her ears strained as she listened closely. The sound of the horses' hooves pounding the road and the rattle of engines made her feel faint. She was terrified, more afraid than she had ever been in her short life and fearful of the looming sorrow. The siege of McAllister's Lane was nigh. "I'm afraid, Papa," were her spoken words.

"It's all right to be afraid, Kat," replied Thomas, staring towards the clamor of the approaching men. "Just don't give them the pleasure of knowing it."

Together, hand in hand, Katie and Thomas McAllister quoted from the first chapter of Joshua. "Be strong and of good courage; be not afraid, neither be thou dismayed, for the Lord thy God is with thee withersoever thou goest."

Screeching to a halt, the pickups whirled into the yard. Horses, breathing hard from their long ride, were reined to a stop. Hooded men, wearing the signature robes of white, sat on the backs of the winded animals. Patiently, the Klansmen waited to receive orders from their leader.

When their leader spoke, his voice, cold and harsh, rang through the darkness like thunder. His sheep, the hooded white men, drank his words like cisterns catching water. "I call out to you, McAllisters. The day of your judgment has arrived!"

Katie shivered. Although afraid, she would never lose her will and strength to resist.

The Klansman continued to bellow, "I urge you to surrender yourselves and surrender the Kings!"

The McAllisters remained silent, unwilling to comply.

"Then you prefer to die?" Impatiently, the leader on horseback waited for a reply.

Katie and Thomas continued to sit stoically. They knew if they raised their guns against them, they would surely die. This time, Katie could not fight her way out. She had to remain passive in order to survive.

"Then die you will! But not before you watch the destruction of your precious McAllister's Lane!"

Thomas slowly stood. Katie flinched. Thomas strained to keep his voice steady. "What do you want from us, and what do you want with the Kings?"

"Jezra and Sadie King are the ma and pa of that colored boy who murdered the O'Hara girl. We've come to rid this county of all blacks with bad blood. As for you, McAllister, we've come to rid this country of white nigger lovers." Narrowed eyes, seen through the slits of the white pointed hood, glared directly at Katie.

Although Katie could not see the face of this cowardly man hiding behind the white hood, she knew him well. He was the man from Texas. She glanced down at the shotgun lying hidden on the porch next to her feet—ready to shoot if necessary.

The depraved man yelled, "Then sit there like stumps on a log! We'll find the Kings even if we have to burn down everything on this place." Fierce, piercing eyes met Katie's. "What do you think of that, Miss McAllister?"

Not so long ago, Katie and Luke had saved Preacher Smith's church from the wrath of this very man and the Klan. There in that church in that small community, once again, she found herself in a state of retribution where she was forced to deal with the sin of an unforgiving and bitter spirit. However, with Preacher Smith's gentle guidance and encouragement, tranquility had overcome feelings of bitterness and hatred once and for all.

In this present time and place, the words of this evil Klansman stabbed at her very core. Nonetheless, she remained unyielding, realizing that God used difficulties and Satan's attacks to build character and faith. Her trust in the Father had deepened, and she thanked Him for every opportunity to grow. Her faith not only delivered her from the past, but *hope* gave her a promise of the future. God's love filled her life and gave her the ability to forgive and to conquer this 'valley' experience and move towards the mountaintop. She knew that her Heavenly Father would not forsake her during this time of her walk in faith.

With one wave of the leader's hand, two men pulled a log off the back of one of the pickups. With long ropes tied to both ends of the log and attached to the horns of their saddles, they made a drag. Pulling the drag between them, they galloped down the rows of sweet potatoes, ripping the lush, green vines from the ground. Several men began to set fire to a cross which they had braced to stand in front of the house. The flames from the cross leaped like the indignant hatred of the scoundrels who ignited it. Others headed for the barn. Flaming torches, tossed on the dry hay, sent a raging blaze leaping up toward the sky.

Katie cringed when she heard the braying of mules in distress. The milk cow and her calf bellowed. Unable to restrain herself anymore, Katie jumped up from her chair.

"I've had enough!" She ran down the steps and out toward the barn. A barn could be rebuilt, but the needless, agonizing death of helpless animals was more than she could bear.

Thomas cried out, "No! Katie, come back!"

It was too late. Katie darted across the yard to save the terrified animals. The man from Texas saw her sprinting towards the barn. He whirled his horse around, digging his heels deep into the animal's side. As he neared Katie, he slowed his mount. With one hand, he pulled her up and laid her across the saddle. Helplessly, Katie kicked and screamed, trying to free herself from the man's strong grasp as he spurred his horse towards the potato house.

Thomas ran to his daughter's aid as fast as he could. As he crossed the yard, one of the hooded Klansmen on horseback spotted him and sent his horse charging. A crashing blow to Thomas's head with the stock of the Klansman's shotgun sent him bowling over. Face down, Thomas's head gushed blood. Motionless, he lay on the cold, hard ground.

From out of nowhere, Jezra bolted out of the darkness of the night! He picked up Thomas's gun and began shooting erratically. Bullets whizzed. One man, then two, went down. The chamber emptied. Swinging the empty gun with all his might, he sent two men sprawling with heads split open by the butt of the gun.

From an unseen assailant's gun, another shot fired. The bullet from the Klansman's gun shot through Jezra's chest. For a brief moment, he stood stoically. He turned to face Katie. Their eyes met. Then Jezra fell to ground.

Katie cried out, "Jezra!"

The Klansman hurled Katie through the door of the potato house. Slamming the door behind him, he stood momentarily, gawking sensually at the woman he lusted for. Katie scrambled to her feet. Slowly, he inched his way towards her, backing her into a corner. Katie's hard slap across his face caused his lip, which she had bitten earlier in the day, to spurt blood. His fingers rubbed his stinging face. As he dabbed the bleeding lip, angrily, he clenched his teeth, snarling like a wild animal about to pounce upon its prey.

Unexpectedly, the man raised his hand. Katie crouched and attempted to cover her face. However, a forceful slap sent her staggering to the floor. Scrambling, she attempted to get on her feet. Blood oozed from her nose and mouth, dripping onto the floor. Then the man's strong hand clamped around her mouth to smother her screams. Katie yanked her head free from the man's grasp and screamed, "Help me!"

"Shut up or I'll kill you!" the man shouted, forcing her mouth shut.

Katie kicked and struggled with all of her strength. However, the attacker slammed her to the floor. Pinning her arms and legs down, he straddled the flailing young woman from McAllister's Lane. A lingering sneer eased across his face. Slowly, he lowered his lips to meet hers. Katie spat; blood splattered. Calmly, he wiped his face with the sleeve of his shirt.

"You are a little fighter, aren't you, Katie McAllister?" He threw his head back as he laughed. "Rosie O'Hara was also a fighter."

Katie gasped. "What do you mean?"

"Your little friend, Rosie O'Hara. She didn't give it up without a fight, either."

"How...how do you know?" she stammered.

"I watched the old hobo rape her."

Although her attempts to fight her way free failed, Katie continued to squirm. "You watched? Why didn't you do something to help her? Why didn't you try to save her?"

"I was too far away. I watched with my binoculars while Creel Burr raped her. When I saw that she had stopped moving, I realized that she must be dead, so I just kept my distance."

Again, Katie strained to free herself, but the man was too strong. Finally, she relented. She wanted to know more, so she coaxed him into talking. Katie asked, "If you knew it was Creel, then why did you allow Son to take the blame?"

"I'm paid by the Klan to incite riots and to stir up problems between the races. I've been trying to get an organization started in this area for a long time. All I did was take advantage of a perfectly good opportunity to get everyone angry enough to side with the Klan. When I saw Creel Burr kill that girl, I knew that I could use it to play into my plan." He cackled. "It was a gruesome sight! But it was the perfect opportunity to get these people around here angry enough to join up with me."

"You're gonna burn in Satan's Hell for this. You know that, don't you?"

"Probably so," he sneered. "And I suppose that I'm fixing to add to my growing list of sins because I'm going to take you,

Katie McAllister." His face neared Katie's. "I'm going to make this little country pumpkin all mine. I want to know what it feels like to take my pleasure from a little spitfire like you."

A hard mouth firmly pressed against Katie's, suffocating her with wet, sloppy kisses. With one hand, he ripped her shirt. Helplessly, Katie kicked and squirmed but to no avail. Desperately, she tried to remove the man as she pushed hard against his persistent body.

All of a sudden, the Klansman's hard and shallow breathing gulped to a stop! He moaned. Ghastly, startled eyes stared briefly into Katie's. Then he collapsed. Katie pushed against the weight of his lifeless body. As she reached around his back, she felt the trickle of warm blood. As she pushed him over to his side, she saw something protruding out of his back. Thrust deep within the man's back was a pitchfork—draining the last breath of life out of the Western man with the silver slide! Katie looked up and into the deadening eyes of the executioner. Standing strong, determined, and emotional was Sadie King!

Chapter 22

A TWIST OF FATE

Clinging tenaciously to each other, Sadie and Katie walked out of the potato house. Devastation was all around them. The buildings were consumed by fire; nothing was spared. The smoke-filled dark sky was illuminated by the brilliance of the roaring, ruinous fire. The wild, frenzied Klansmen were scattered. The appalling, cowardly men, hiding behind white sheets and pointed hoods, were brutally slaughtering the mules and the cows that did not perish in the blazing inferno beneath the falling timbers of the barn. The bloodthirsty men searched intensively for Katie and Sadie. Their intent was to hang the two women from McAllister's Lane.

Suddenly, Sadie spotted Jezra lying motionless on the ground! She dashed to his side. Kneeling beside her husband, she cradled him in her arms, crying softly as she gently rocked his lifeless body back and forth.

It was then that Katie spied her father, who also was lying on the cold ground, not moving. As she sprinted to Thomas, a Klansman spotted her running across the yard. Suddenly, he pulled hard back on the reins, spinning his horse around, and raced for Katie. Distracting the dangerous rider, an alarming noise rang from out of the darkness of McAllister's Lane. A loud clamor of automobile horns blowing and the sound of men shouting rose above the bedlam.

Through smoke-filled eyes and burning tears, Katie stared down the road. At first, she could barely see through the darkness. Then, out of the dust and through the clouds of smoke came the figures and faces of familiar men. Bustling to a stop, they bolted out of the vehicles that carried them to the rescue of Katie McAllister and Sadie King. Friends and neighbors who had once been manipulated by the Klansman from Texas to play a part in the execution of Son King were now racing to the women's defense! Men who had once feared Katie McAllister had grown to respect and honor her courage and tenacity. This group of men was now coming to liberate McAllister's Lane and its occupants from their doom. They would fight for Katie McAllister no matter what the cost.

Buster Reese, the neighbor Katie saved from the interment death of a quicksand bed, was the first to hit the ground running. Gallantly, he charged a Klansman with a pick, swinging it with all of his might. The force of the pick sent the man to his knees, where he died a short but agonizing death.

The one-eared Mr. McKinnon, along with his sons, Jamison and Addison, were next to vault from their vehicle. Swiftly extracting their pistols from their holsters, they carefully took aim. Shots rang out in the darkness of the night. One, then two Klansmen suffered the mighty sting of death.

The horsemen pulled the bits hard on the frightened horses' mouths. They whirled and whinnied as their riders turned them around and around, looking for an escape route. Whiskey Jones lunged at a horse and its rider. Springing up on the horse's side, he grabbed the man sitting atop the big animal. Relentlessly, the Klansman held to the saddle horn and clamped his legs tighter around the animal's girth. Suddenly, both horse and man fell to the ground. The Klansman's leg, pinned under the weight of the big sorrel, was helplessly trapped. The vulnerable man could not escape the deadly pelting blows of Whiskey's fist.

Jackson Buford, who Katie helped put to sleep for Doc Owens to perform an appendectomy, was also among the rescuers. Standing on the back of a pickup, he sent shots from his rifle whizzing by the heads of Klansmen with only near misses.

Mr. O'Hara, the father of Rosie, raped and strangled to death by Creel Burr, opened fire on a Klansman who was shooting wildly through the crowd. That particular Klansman's bullets never found their targets. Nevertheless, Mr. O'Hara's bullet was buried deep into the chest of the man, where it was specifically aimed. The man clasped his wound. Eyes glazed as he stared in bewilderment. Then, slowly, they closed in death.

One Klansman saw an opening. Quickly, he turned his horse and spurred the confused animal to run past the automobiles down the lane. However, the lane that led to the McAllister farm would not serve as an outlet for the men who had come to destroy her. Before the driven animal reached its exit, he stumbled in an old pothole, throwing his rider to the hard ground below, hitting his head on a rock. Blood gushed. The fallen Klansman lay lifeless. For generations, this land, preserved and nourished by a family who upheld the rights and equality of all men, now lay wasted, charred, and desolate. But in her devastation, McAllister's Lane did her part trying to save herself from those who had come to destroy her.

As quickly as they came to kill, they died. Nine Klansmen lay dead with only one escape. Slyly, discreetly, that man disappeared into the obscurity of the dark night.

Suddenly, from where Thomas was lying, there was a low, soft moan. It was Thomas! He was alive! Carefully, Katie lifted her father's head and gently held it in her lap. As she looked at the large gash on her father's head, she cried out, "Papa, please don't die! If only Doc were here, he could fix you, and you would be all better."

From behind, a familiar, reassuring voice said, "I *am* here, Katie." The old family doctor, who had rallied the men to go to Katie's aid, stood above the wounded man and the frightened young woman. Kneeling beside Katie and her father, he examined the cut on Thomas's head. "Gonna have a headache for a while, but a few stitches should heal that right up."

"Doc," sobbed Katie, "where did you come from?"

"I've been sitting over there in my car watching the whole thing," Doc said as he motioned towards his automobile. "Took a Hippocratic oath to save lives, not take them…but didn't mind this one bit. Those hoodlums got what was coming to them."

"How did you know the Klan was coming here tonight?" Katie asked.

Doc began to bandage Thomas's badly cut head. Nonchalantly, he answered Katie. "That young man of yours came crawling into town."

"Luke? Crawling?"

"Yep. It was your Luke all right. Said as the train pulled out from the station, he looked back to get one last glimpse of you. He saw those men encountering you and knew that it meant trouble. He recognized one of the Klansmen." Doc tied the bandage snugly. He stood, brushing his hands. "Said that he knew the one he recognized to be the leader of the Klan, the man you and Luke stopped from burning Preacher Smith's church."

Thomas moaned and tried to get up.

"Now, lay still, Thomas," ordered Doc. "I'll get some men to help me carry you down to Sadie's house. I'll get you sewed up in no time."

Katie was exasperated. Her head whirled with questions. "Doc! Tell me about Luke."

"Well, the boy couldn't get the conductor to stop the train, so he jumped off."

"Jumped off a moving train?" asked Katie. "Was he hurt?"

"Heck, yeah, he was hurt! Wouldn't you be hurt if you jumped off a moving train?" Doc joked. "He broke one foot and sprained the other. And if that wasn't enough, he dislocated his shoulder." He smiled. "And the dang boy crawled back to town! That's love for ya!"

"Oh, Doc." Katie couldn't bear to hear anything else. "Where is he? Where is Luke?"

The old country doctor pushed his spectacles down and peered down his nose. "I didn't tell you? Guess I forgot." Doc pointed to his automobile. "He's a-sittin' in the backseat of that car over there."

Katie sprang to her feet and ran towards Luke. She had almost reached the automobile when a shot was fired from out of the darkness. The bullet hit the ground only a few feet in front of her. She froze, as did everyone else.

"Katie McAllister!" a booming voice yelled from the murky shadows. The Klansman who had escaped earlier was hiding and waiting for an opportunity to shoot Katie. "The Klan came here to kill you tonight. Say good-bye."

Luke pushed himself up from the backseat of Doc's car. Helplessly, he looked into the face of the love of his life. Their eyes locked. Both realized that this was the end.

Suddenly, from out of nowhere, another lone shot was fired. Katie closed her eyes. She waited to die, but there was no pain.

She felt for blood, but there was none. There was no sting of death. Slowly, she turned. From out of the shadows walked the Klansman. At a snail's pace, he desperately tried to put one foot in front of the other. Slowly, he raised his hand and reached outward for Katie. Without taking his eyes from hers, he went down to his knees. Then, slumping over, he fell to the ground. The lone Klansman heaved and took his last and final breath.

Whirling around, Katie's eyes frantically searched the crowd to see who had shot the Klansman. Standing near Thomas was Doc Owens. In his hand was the gun that Thomas had dropped in his pursuit to save Katie.

Everyone was aghast. Nevertheless, Doc never even flinched. Cautiously, he laid the gun back down on the ground. "Like I said, I took an oath to save lives…even if it means having to take one."

Chapter 23

OUT OF THE ASHES

The friends and neighbors who came to the rescue of the inhabitants of McAllister's Lane stood silently in the darkness. Slowly, the first rays of the morning sun glistened across the dismal sky. As they began to walk among the devastation and the dead, they spoke softly among themselves. Attempting to absorb and contemplate the previous night's events, they pondered what actions to take next.

Mr. O'Hara spoke first. "I think the best thing for us to do is go get the law."

Buster Reese, standing nearby, understood the significance of what had happened on McAllister's Lane and the consequences. He was quick to object. "And I think that's crazy. We all know that the only law in the backwoods is the law we make." He looked around for the others to agree. "Besides, if we bring the law into this, then the hanging of Son King will be found out for sure. We promised each other a long time ago that all of us would keep that a secret." He paused. "If the law finds out about that night, *we* might all hang."

The other men looked around at one another and nodded in agreement. One of the McKinnon boys asked, "What are we gonna do with their bodies? Don't you think that these men have families who'll be wondering where they are?"

Again Buster was quick to answer. "Those men are from way off. All of 'em were from out of state. Anyway, if they have family, they probably don't even know where they are. Usually, men in their line of work never make it back home alive. A lot of risks come with the job."

Someone from the crowd asked, "Where are we going to bury them? Someone will find their graves for sure."

Buster squinted. "I know just the place. And we don't even have to dig a grave."

Still undecided, they agreed to receive counsel from their wise friend Doc Owens, whose knowledge and wisdom rivaled that of a Philadelphia lawyer. Doc was at the Kings' house with the McAllisters and Luke. Sadie was also there, bathing and dressing Jezra for his burial.

The men walked down the lane to the Kings' home and gathered around the front porch. Doc walked out, sat down, and rocked back in a chair. "Well?"

"How's that boy Luke, and what about Thomas?" McKinnon asked.

Doc took a draw from his pipe and crossed his arms. "Gonna make it. Gonna be fine. Thomas will have a headache for a while, and Luke won't be doing much walking on those feet until they heal."

Mr. O'Hara cleared his throat before speaking. "Doc, us boys been thinking this thing out." He scratched his chin. "We're a thinkin' that it might be best if we never tell of last night. Let's bury it and forget it along with those men."

Doc nodded his head in agreement. A true leader, honorable and inspiring, he indicated his feelings on all the past atrocities. "Yeah, boys, and I'm thinking you might just be right. And when we bury them, let's bury with them all the bad memories that ever happened here on McAllister's Lane. What happened here was compounded by a lot of animosity and hatred. What happened to Son King was ruthless and cruel. It was an act of harassment, intimidation, and violence."

Doc stood and hit his fist against the porch post. "And, we allowed strangers to come into our community and destroy this peaceful, God-fearing place. We allowed them to execute their white supremacist rituals and acts of violence. We can't change what happened or bring back the past to undo. We can't undo what is already done."

Doc pointed down the lane towards the McAllister home place and farm, still smoldering from the previous night's fire. "But there is something that we can do. Out of the ashes can come a change for the black race and hope for a new beginning. No longer will we welcome a society for bigotries. We will never again allow the Klan to get a foothold in our community. We will break the back of racial injustice, and it *will* start here."

The crowd cheered.

At that moment, Sadie walked around the corner of the house. She overheard the men talking with Doc on the porch. In her hand was the most grotesque object Doc and the others had ever seen! She had retrieved the object from the flour barrel that was in the corner of the back porch. Some time ago, Katie had attempted to look inside this same barrel. On that particular day, Sadie panicked and, to Katie's surprise, screamed to stop her from looking inside. Sadie's past actions were now made clear. Packed inside the barrel with packing salt used to cure fatback and fish was a reminder of *her* hatred.

Sadie slowly walked, holding the object out from her body by its hair. It was the distorted and salt-cured decapitated head of Creel Burr! When Creel was struck by the locomotive on the train trestle, his body was thrown off the tracks into the Flint! On that horrific day, after Katie left, Jezra swam out into the river to retrieve Creel's body. How Creel's head was decapitated, no one but Jezra would ever know. What was brought to light was that Creel Burr's head was packed it in a barrel where it had remained until this day.

The men, stunned and speechless, stood horror-struck.

Not Sadie! Proudly, she displayed the shriveled, ghastly head of the hobo who had ransacked and preyed on the land and people of McAllister's Lane. Standing tall and proud, she beamed. "And when we bury the Klan, let's bury what's left of this man with them. Let's put 'em all in the ground together and bury 'em deep! Let our God bring beauty out of the destruction. Let Him bring joy out of the mourning and praise out of the heaviness in our hearts! It is time we learned to find comfort for our pain and peace in the midst of our strife. Right here and now, let's allow the trials we have endured to be the key to the door of a greater hope and faith—for all people of all skins! Like the bird escaping from the hunter's snare, let's be free of this."

All nodded, praising and embracing the woman of color who showed more heart than any woman, of any color, they knew. This exemplary lady was an encouragement for them to break down walls and barriers of the past and erect new ones that would no longer divide the races.

Later that morning, Katie and Doc, along with the others, stood next to the burial place of the Klansmen from Texas and the head of Creel Burr. Rocks tied securely around the dead men weighed down their bodies. Creel's head, also tied to rocks, would never rise from the gloomy depths of its grave. One by one, the Klansmen were cast into the murky, shifting sands of the quicksand bed that not so long ago had almost pulled Buster Reese to his death.

Katie stood at the very spot where she had helped Buster out of the pit. Next into the pit was the decapitated head of Creel Burr. Eyes that never closed in death seemed to focus on Katie as they slowly descended. Quietly, she watched as each man, one by one, sank deeper and deeper into the dark belly of the murky sands. The last man to descend to his morbid grave was the leader of the Klansman, the man who wore the silver bolo slide. Bigotry bubbled as the man from Texas slowly slid into his final resting place.

Katie turned to Doc and said, "I never even knew his name. All I ever knew was that he was from Texas."

Doc turned to Katie. He lovingly wrapped his arms around her trembling shoulders. "That's all you ever need to know."

Weeks later, a deputy sheriff was sent to McAllister's Lane to question the disappearance of the men who had come to destroy Katie and her family. It seemed that the hotel clerk reported that they never returned for their possessions. As the deputy sheriff pulled up to the McAllisters' homestead, he was stupefied at the sight he saw. All that remained were the charred remnants of the big house and barn that once graced this small South Georgia farm.

Slowly, he stepped out of his pickup. Scratching his head in disbelief, he walked around, looking for signs of people. There were none. Suddenly, he saw a bright, shiny object half buried in the dirt and mingled among the ashes. He kicked it up with his boot, examined it, and put it inside his pocket.

As he got back in his pickup, he looked over his shoulder one more time at the remains of the place called McAllister's Lane. It was sad, he thought, that this beautiful place, which had once served as the home of the McAllisters and Kings, had been ruthlessly destroyed.

As the deputy drove down the lane, he passed the McAllister family cemetery and noticed a freshly dug grave. Carved in a wooden cross was the name 'Jezra.' Further down the lane, he glanced over at the little sharecropper's house where the Kings once lived. It was boarded up and seemingly empty.

As the deputy sheriff reached the entrance of the lane, he spied Mr. O'Hara standing in the vicinity of a charred stump where a lone tree once stood. He slowed, then stopped. Getting out of his pickup, he called out, "Howdy, Mr. O'Hara!"

Mr. O'Hara, staring off into the distance, did not respond.

Walking up to Mr. O'Hara, the deputy sheriff kindly extended his hand. "What caused that tree to burn down? Lightning?"

"Don't know."

The deputy sheriff paused and then said, "Ain't seen any strangers around here, have you?"

"Nope."

The deputy sheriff scratched his chin. "What happened to the home place down at the end of McAllister's Lane?"

"Caught fire. That's all I know."

The deputy sheriff glanced down the lane. "What happened to Katie and Thomas McAllister? And to Sadie King? Where have they gone?"

Mr. O'Hara gazed directly into the inquisitive deputy sheriff's eyes. "Ain't got no idea, but I hope it's a better place than around here."

The deputy sheriff fumbled in his pocket and pulled out the shiny object that he had kicked up from the ashes back at the McAllisters' farm. He held it up into the sunlight. It glistened. He looked at Mr. O'Hara. "Don't know what this little thing is, do you, Mr. O'Hara?"

Emotionless, Mr. O'Hara shrugged his shoulders.

The deputy sheriff said, "Sorta looks like one of those bolo slides that cowboys put on those string things they wear around their necks."

For a brief moment, Mr. O'Hara stared at the shiny silver object and then recognized it. "Don't know what it is," he lied. "Don't look like squat to me."

"You're right," replied the deputy sheriff. "It doesn't look like squat." With that said, he reared back and threw the silver object into the air as hard as he could. It landed on the ground near the road, rolling and bumping along until it finally came to a stop at the base of the charred stump. It landed at the base of the tree once used to hang Son King—the Judgment Tree!

"Well," said the deputy sheriff, "if you see or hear from the McAllisters, tell 'em that I would like to talk to 'em."

Mr. O'Hara nodded. The deputy sheriff climbed in his pickup and drove away.

Mr. O'Hara walked over to the place where Son King had died. He stooped down and picked up the silver slide that had come to rest at the base of the charred stump. Briefly, he held the slide in his hand before hurling it as far as he could. The bright, shiny bolo slide flew through the air, twisting and turning and glistening in the sun. "And this thing ain't squat."

Mr. O'Hara stepped out into the road and looked down towards McAllister's homeplace. For a moment, he thought he heard the old dinner bell ringing and signaling for the McAllisters and Kings to come home. A gentle wind rustled. Leaves whirled and twisted. The branches in the tall trees above waved back and forth as if the presence of a spirit were moving among them.

Mr. O'Hara stood silent and still. Quietly, he listened and watched the tree branches swish and sway. "Son," he whispered, "is that you? You can go home, now, Son. All is well here. Go home, Son. Go on home to your mansion in the sky."

At that moment, a calmness overcame the place where the trees swayed and the leaves rustled. Slowly, a comforting and reassuring peace gently fell across this mystic land called McAllister's Lane. Peace was now Son King's, and now he was at home, at home in his mansion in the sky.

CPSIA information can be obtained at www.ICGtesting.com
Printed in the USA
LVOW06s0034221214

419697LV00021B/31/P